"Now, WE ALREADY KNOW YOU LIKE SEX, SO LET'S move along to old movies. Do you have a favorite?" Noah asked.

"Ah, wait a second. *We* don't know that I like sex," Mich retorted.

"Sure we do," he said, brushing a finger along the soft skin of her arm. "*Casablanca*, right?"

"No, that's not my favorite." She snatched her arm away. "And how do *we* know that I like sex?"

He chuckled. "You're not exactly a subtle woman, Michelin."

"What's that supposed to mean?"

"It means," he said, "that every time I get this close to you, your eyes get a little darker, almost black, very mysterious. Your breath comes a little faster." He ran his finger down the column of her neck to the pulse skipping along at the bottom of it. "Your heart beats a little faster and your skin gets warmer."

"Stop that! I'm driving. And you're dead wrong. I feel fine." A quick eye to the speedometer, and she took her foot off the gas to slow everything down.

"You do indeed," he said, sliding his finger back up her neck, under her chin, and across her lower lip. "So soft. Warm. Very fine. Downright irresistible."

"You'd better stop that," she muttered, but to her ears it sounded like *more, more, more.* Then she pulled the car over and punched the brake to the floor. . . .

WHAT ARE *LOVESWEPT* ROMANCES?

They are stories of true romance and touching emotion. We believe those two very important ingredients are constants in our highly sensual and very believable stories in the LOVE-SWEPT line. Our goal is to give you, the reader, stories of consistently high quality that may sometimes make you laugh, sometimes make you cry, but are always fresh and creative and contain many delightful surprises within their pages.

Most romance fans read an enormous number of books. Those they truly love, they keep. Others may be traded with friends and soon forgotten. We hope that each LOVESWEPT romance will be a treasure—a "keeper." We will always try to publish

LOVE STORIES YOU'LL NEVER FORGET
BY AUTHORS YOU'LL ALWAYS REMEMBER

The Editors

Loveswept ® 894

ONE ON ONE

MARY KAY McCOMAS

BANTAM BOOKS
NEW YORK · TORONTO · LONDON · SYDNEY · AUCKLAND

This book was titled by Ben McComas.

ONE ON ONE

A Bantam Book / July 1998

ISBN 0-553-44690-8

Published simultaneously in the United States and Canada

Bantam Books are published by Bantam Books, a division of Bantam Dou-
bleday Dell Publishing Group, Inc. Its trademark, consisting of the words
"Bantam Books" and the portrayal of a rooster, is Registered in U.S.
Patent and Trademark Office and in other countries. Marca Registrada.
Bantam Books, 1540 Broadway, New York, New York 10036.

PRINTED IN THE UNITED STATES OF AMERICA

OPM   10 9 8 7 6 5 4 3 2 1

ONE

It was his nature to be honest and forthright.

Over the years he'd taught himself to be prudent and thrifty as well, so it went against his grain to shred the nearly new fan belt in the rented compact with a metal file. The spare tire he'd thrown in a ditch a hundred miles east would weigh on his conscience for some time to come. But at this point it seemed as necessary to shred the fan belt and toss the tire as it was to be dishonest and misleading.

A day, two at the most, was all he would need to get a clear picture of the circumstances. Then he could come clean, tell everyone who he was and why he'd come, and they'd welcome him with open arms.

Maybe he should have brought something to drink, he thought, touching his dry tongue to his drier lips. There was no telling how long he'd have to wait, having stranded himself in the vast Nevada desert. He hoped that the emergency-road-service operator could follow simple instructions. If that overly calm, soft-spoken representative called the wrong towing service, there would be hell to pay—bet the rent on it, he nodded decisively.

Heat waves rose up from the asphalt all around him. The sun licked fire on his face and neck. He slipped the loosely knotted neck tie off and tossed it through the car window to join the suit jacket and the cellular telephone on the seat. Posing as a traveling businessman to appear more pathetic and helpless had been pointless, a clear case of overkill, he decided. A man on vacation in jeans and a T-shirt would have looked just as pitiful and disabled in this heat. Hell, if he were truly stranded, a three-hundred-pound truck driver in a tank top and shorts with a cold six-pack under his arm would have tears in his eyes. . . .

Come to think of it, who in their right mind *wouldn't* procure fluids prior to embarking on a trip across a desert?

He leaned back against the driver's-side door and wiped his brow with a stiff white handkerchief, his scattered thoughts shifting back to his prime objective.

Man's inhumanity to man was what he'd dedicated his life to preventing, which made it as sad as it was ironic that he hadn't known what was happening in his own home.

He closed his eyes and let his head fall forward on his neck. What would it be like to speed down this very highway on a motorcycle? he wondered. Heart free, the wind in his hair? With no responsibilities, an underdeveloped sense of duty, and a staunch passion to live—to feel, to taste, to see life second by second?

A new pain tugged at the delicate scar tissue of long-healed wounds, and he breathed in the hot dry air, held it in his lungs until they ached, then slowly released it.

He was partly to blame. As much as he wanted to plead his innocence, ignorance wasn't a good enough excuse. He should have been there. He should have paid more attention. He should have suspected.

A movement in the east caught his attention. His expensive oxford shirt was pasted to his back, wet and sticky. He was definitely going to make a wretched first impression, he thought, a wry smile curving his lips as he shaded his eyes to look down the road.

The blur of heat waves was so dense that he didn't see the truck until it was almost upon him, despite the fact that the landscape was as flat and dry as a tortilla.

In order to be all the things he prided himself most on being—honest, forthright, prudent, and thrifty—he knew it was necessary to be prepared. Going into this particular situation, he felt he was sufficiently prepared to accept whatever came his way.

The tow truck, for instance, was not new and shiny but old, rusted, and missing the right front fender. This didn't surprise him. The Albee Trucking & Towing logo on the door was bashed in, chipped, and faded. That was a relief. He now knew he could count on his rental company. A woman was driving. He'd been hoping she would be.

The truck came to a loud rattling stop in front of him, and he got his first good look at her. Michelin was her name. She wore a baseball cap with the word BOSS across the bill, her dark hair pulled through the hole in the back like a ponytail.

Dark hair. A brunette?

Odd. His brother, Eric, had always been so definite about his preference for blondes. He used to say, "Brunettes think too much. That's why *you* like them, remember? Me? I'll take a cute little blonde with long legs and a good sense of humor any day of the week." Then he'd grin wickedly. But he'd been . . . what? Maybe seventeen or eighteen at the time. Young. Immature. Cocky.

Well, be that as it may, the fact that she was a brunette wasn't an earth-shattering surprise—but the rest of her face was. It belonged on a dairy poster. Healthy was the first word that came to him. She had a glowing, sun-kissed complexion, an uncomplicated nose, and a large mouth with soft, luscious-looking lips that were smiling at him, showing him a row of white even teeth. Shaded glasses dangled from her fingertips and large, thoughtful dark eyes were taking him in and evaluating him at ten times the speed of his own.

"Are you waiting for me?" she called through the truck's open side window. "Or the next bus? Which, if you're lucky, should pass this way in about"—she looked at her watch—"oh, four or five hours, depending on the special at Eddy's Diner today. If it's meat loaf or salmon cakes, it'll be here on time. If it's the chicken special, you might be here a while."

"No. No," he said, intrigued by the reaction in his knees to her slightly raspy voice. "I sent for you. Actually, I called the rental company. I'm hoping they sent you."

"Is your name Thomas?"

"Yes," he said, and where he might have smiled happily at being rescued, he smiled instead to hide any guilt that might be lurking in his eyes. "Please tell me you're not a mirage and that you know more about cars than I do. Tell me you can fix it."

She laughed. "Well, I'm sure not a mirage, and I'll give it my best shot. How's that?"

"That sounds good."

It was part of her routine to stop the truck with the motor running and have a check-it-out conversation with would-be customers. She had good instincts about people, and it seemed that the more inane the subject of the initial dialogue, the more she could tell about the person.

This man, for instance, knew she knew he wasn't waiting for a bus and that he didn't care what the special at Eddy's Diner was, but he was friendly enough and well-mannered enough to play along with her. That he was glad to see her was clear in his facial expression, but that he had no intention of taking advantage of the fact that she was a woman was apparent in his respectful, appreciative manner of speaking. And, of course, her job was always easier when she didn't have to deal with amateur mechanics.

This man was okay, she decided, taking her foot off the brake as she slipped her dark glasses back on.

Then digressing, just a bit, she noted he was also breath-clogging, heart-halting, skin-tingling, palm-sweatingly handsome! A tall man with broad shoulders and not even a hint of a paunch above his belt, he had dark wavy hair and sharp keen eyes that were probably green but could also be brown. She found herself itching to get close enough to find out.

It was his smile, however—wide and charming and a

little bit devilish—that sent her pulse racing. She took another quick peek at it through the rearview mirror.

The name Mr. Thomas was still ringing strangely in his ears while she pulled the truck ahead of the rental car along the side of the road. He stepped out onto the asphalt as she used the rear- and side-view mirrors to back it expertly to within a foot of the front fender and turned off the engine.

It wasn't the first time he'd thought it unusual for a woman to be operating a towing service—dangerous even, now that he'd seen how empty and isolated this stretch of highway was. But she was clearly no novice. Every movement she made was a study in confidence.

She gathered papers and heavy work gloves off the seat next to her, opened the door, and step-hopped to the ground.

Noah could feel himself melting into the soft, steaming asphalt beneath his feet. Visions of Daisy Mae blinked through his mind as he took in the long expanse of shapely leg between cutoff jeans and the work boots on her feet. The sleeveless cotton shirt she had tied at her waist wasn't filled to quite the same magnitude, and, of course, the hair was the wrong color, but these were minor details and did nothing to ease the hard lump of air stuck firmly in his throat.

"What seems to be your problem?" she asked.

"What?"

"The problem? With your car?"

"Oh," he said, collecting himself quickly. "Ah . . . I don't know."

Her stride was long and slow as she walked back to the car. She nodded and smiled and squeezed the gloves tight in her hand. Something wild and crazy was stirring inside her, jingling her nerves and prickling her skin.

"You're not out of gas, are you?" she asked, her tone light, almost teasing.

This was a good sign. She liked him. He could tell.

"No. I was careful to fill up the tank back in Gypsum. The man there said it would be a hundred and twenty miles to the next gas station. I was pretty sure I had enough, but I had him top it off to make sure." A pause. "He checked the water in the radiator too," he added, wanting to impress her with his clear thinking, his foresight and vigilance . . . with anything really.

"Aw. That explains it," she said, setting the papers and gloves on the back of the truck and raising the hood over the sedan's engine with a quick glance in his direction.

"It does?" He stepped closer. "Explains what?"

"Why you look so familiar to me," she said, concentrating hard on the engine, looking for the most obvious problems before going through each system in detail. "The man at the station back in Gypsum is my dad. I must have seen you while you were there." She frowned. "But I don't recall seeing this car before."

His heart sank to the pit of his stomach. He looked familiar to her?

"Oh. Well . . . don't all cars start to look alike after a while?" He stepped up beside the car to peer in at the engine with her—as if he knew this end of an automobile as well as he knew the other. "I mean, wouldn't a blue . . . ah . . . Chevy you saw today look exactly like a blue Chevy you saw a month ago?" He was the world's worst liar. He really was. His face was hot and his hands were clammy. Couldn't she tell he was lying?

"Aw," she said again with satisfaction, breaking in on his stammering as if she hadn't been listening. "I think this might be your lucky day, Mr. Thomas. You snapped your belt here," she said, giving a hefty tug and pulling the belt out of the engine like a rubber snake. "I might be able to replace this and have you back on the road in less than an hour."

"An hour?" After he'd gone to all this trouble? After he'd sweat blood deciding which belt to cut? After he'd made all these plans? Damn, maybe he was going to have to flatten that tire after all. He looked to see several spares on the back of her truck and cursed them.

"Sure," she said, frowning over the belt, examining it. "This happens all the time because of the heat." She paused. "This *is* a rental, right?"

"Ah . . . yes. Yes, it is. Why do you ask?" he said, feigning concern.

She shook her head. "You may want to show someone this belt when you return the car." She handed it to him. "Normal wear and tear affects the whole belt. That one's like new except for where it snapped."

"Hmmph." He was studying the belt, sweating profusely, and feeling guilty as hell. Seems he wasn't any good at sabotage either.

"If you'll fill out this form for me, I can get started," she said, seeming not to give the belt another thought as she handed him a clipboard with a double-copy document on it and a ballpoint pen hanging by a string. After a sharp look, she added, "There's water in the cooler on the front seat. Help yourself."

The relief in his smile came naturally and for more than one reason. She wasn't going to ask any questions, she had water, and she didn't seem to mind that he was acting like an idiot.

She turned then, walking back toward the front of the truck, and that's when he saw it—the military-issue Colt .45 stuffed into the waistband of her shorts against her spine. He wasn't much of a mechanic, but he'd had weapons training. And that little piece of mayhem explained at least part of the woman's confident air. It could easily blow a tree in half.

It also—and he had *no* idea where this thought came from—was the sexiest thing he'd ever seen a woman wear.

"Have you ever had to use that thing?" he asked, more than a little curious.

She glanced over her shoulder, and he motioned with his eyes to the gun. She grinned, and his heart fluttered in his chest.

"Nope," she said, reaching into the cab of the truck for a parts catalog. He was looking her over, a common enough experience in her life, but it usually didn't make her want to giggle. She kept her back to him as she opened the book on the seat and ran her finger down one page after another. "I don't stop if I don't feel easy about it, and I wear the gun in plain sight to ward off any second thoughts someone might be having." She found what she was looking for and leaned closer to the page, reading. "A couple of times," she said, closing the book and tossing it back inside, "I've had to wave it around in the air, to get a drunk's attention, but I've never actually had to fire it."

He watched her climb onto the truck bed and open a large metal box. She wasn't that big a woman, physically. She was on the tall side and looked strong enough, with smooth, defined muscles in her upper arms—the kind that came from daily exertion not a gym. She had capable-looking hands and firm, toned leg muscles.

"*Could* you shoot it?" he asked, intrigued, suspecting the kick from the Colt would knock her flat. "If you had to, could you?"

She stopped rummaging in the metal box to give him a thoughtful look.

"Could I or would I? There's a difference."

She squinted through her dark sunglasses to study him, and doing the same in her direction, he said, "Yes."

A slow smile came to her expression. She liked his directness.

"Yes," she repeated, without a hint of doubt, before returning to the contents of the box. "Wouldn't it be stupid to carry it around, not knowing how or when to use it?"

Just that simply, without rancor or insult, she was telling him that he was free to think anything he liked about her—good or bad, flattering or otherwise—but it would be very foolish of him to believe she was helpless.

Noah, however, had discovered weeks ago that she wasn't helpless, and he was still curious about the gun.

"What I meant was"—he attempted an air of casual conversation by filling out the reimbursement form as he spoke—"wouldn't a smaller-caliber gun be easier for you to handle? Give you better control? I know something about guns, and that one's . . . pretty heavy duty."

Once again, she smiled easily, and he was glad he had looked up in time to catch it.

"It is," she agreed, retrieving two fan belts from the collection she kept inside the box, reading the cardboard band around each. "But when I do something, I like to do it well. And . . . I'm sort of sentimental about this gun. My husband gave it to me."

Then it *was* the same gun he'd given Eric all those years ago . . . and she wasn't averse to talking about him.

"I'm sure it puts his mind at ease knowing you're carrying it out here with you," he said.

"I guess so," she said, tossing both belts back into the box, looking very unhappy. "We have a little problem here, Mr. Thomas. I don't have the right size belt to fit this car. I don't even have one that'll do till you get to Warm Springs."

He really wished she'd stop calling him Mr. Thomas. He hadn't known it would grate on his nerves every time he heard it.

She jumped lightly to the ground in front of him. Casually, she slipped her right hand into her back pocket. The cotton shirt pulled tight across her breasts, and Noah held his breath, hoping she would continue to speak. He couldn't, there wasn't a thought left in his head.

"I'll call and see if we have one in stock and then someone can run it out to us," she said. He thought of the nail and hammer in the trunk of the car, and how he could get to them without her seeing. "But if we don't, you're going to have to decide if you want me to tow you back to Gypsum, where you might have to wait a day or two for us to get it in, or if you'd rather have me tow you into Warm Springs or even Tonopah, where they're more likely to have the right size belt. But then I'd have to charge you for the extra towing, plus my trip back to Gypsum."

When he was slow to respond, not wanting to appear too eager to return to Gypsum with her, she went on, "I'm really sorry about this. I hate to have to tow you anywhere, it's such a simple thing to fix. There's no getting around a service charge, but I could have saved you a lot of time if I'd had the right belt."

Shamefully, this amused him. "It's not your fault," he said, feeling another twinge of guilt for distressing her. "Like you said, these things happen. And if you don't have one in stock, you can tow me back to Gypsum, I think. I'm in no hurry."

"Oh," she said. Unexpectedly addlepated, she wished she was wearing a dress, a slinky dress, cut high and low . . . a slinky red dress. . . . "Good. Most folks who come through here are in a rush to get . . . through. It's the desert," she said with a shrug, walking off to the front of the truck once more. "Makes people feel like they have to get from one end of it to the other as fast as they can, before they die out here, stranded and alone." She laughed softly. "It's funny, but I guess if you're not used to it, being completely alone can make you a little crazy."

But she was used to it, he could tell. She was as comfortable in her own company as she would be in a room full of friends—as she was with a stranger on a deserted highway.

She left the door open after climbing inside the cab of the truck to call Gypsum on the radio. Noah finished filling out the papers, signing *N* and *T* with a squiggle behind it that could have just as easily read Tessler as Thomas, and handed them in to her silently, noting the cooler on the other side of the vehicle.

". . . I won't put the chains on till you know for sure," she was telling someone when he opened the rider's side door. "And Eric?" Some static on the radio. "Will you step on it? It's hot out here."

Reaching for a bottle of water, Noah's arm stopped mid-motion inside the cooler. He knew about Eric Tessler Albee, reported to be age fourteen, solid student, basketball enthusiast, no arrest record, dime-sized brandywine birthmark on his left shoulder. But hearing his name spoken out loud, and realizing it was *him* on the other end of the radio, was like a sudden slap in the face.

Eric Tessler Albee was real.

He looked at the woman, Eric's mother, and found that she'd removed her glasses again and was watching him. He quickly offered her a bottle of water, to which she shook her head no, then smiled at him.

"Got another fainter on your hands?" came a young male voice amid the crackling and snapping on the radio.

Her smile broadened to a grin, and without looking away, she said, "No. Maybe not, but let's not take any chances, okay?"

She held the microphone with both hands in her lap

and sighed. It was several seconds more before the next message came across. "Don't go anywhere."

Her face lit up brighter than the sun, and then she chuckled. She shook her head and glanced over at him, her eyes sparkling with amusement, glowing with love and happiness.

"Kids," she said simply.

He could only nod and turn his attention to drinking deeply from the water bottle, worried that he might choke. If she had ever smiled at his brother like that, then his actions during the last year of his life were easily explained. What nineteen-year-old boy could resist a face like that? What wouldn't he give up to see it on a daily basis?

When he thought he could speak coherently, he stated the obvious, hoping to glean more information.

"Yours, I take it?"

"Mmmm," she affirmed nodding, still smiling, still amused. "He's made it his life's ambition to drive me slowly insane, I think."

"Must be a teenager."

She laughed. "For two years now. He's fourteen. Do you have children that age?"

"No. But most everyone I know does."

"They're a breed in themselves, teenagers," she said with the authority only a parent of one could exercise. "They're either the most wonderful and interesting things in the world or the most frustrating. I've developed a real"—she shook the mike in her right hand, looking for the proper word—"kinship with my dad over the past few years. He put up with four teenagers, and he's still alive to talk about it."

They both chuckled at that, and became aware that their conversation was heading easily in a personal direction. They were no longer tow person and strandee, but more explicitly a woman and a man with a budding interest in one another.

"Mom?" came Eric's voice again. "Was that a two-five-six-oh-seven-eight-oh or a two-five-six-oh-seven-eight-one?"

"Um . . . hang on. I can't remember now."

"Well, it doesn't really matter, we don't have either one. And the only other six rib we have is too long." Noah released a breath he hadn't realized he was holding. His guardian star was still shining on him. "You towing it over to Charlie's place or bringing it home?"

"Home, but have Granddad check with Charlie before he calls the distributor. Maybe Lou Garrett in Tonopah too. We may still be able to save this man some time."

"Okay," he said.

"I'm really sorry about this, Mr. Thomas." She hung the cord of the microphone over a knob on the radio. "Are you sure you wouldn't rather go to Warm Springs?"

"Positive. You know, I've never met anyone as reluctant to make money as you seem to be. Where I come from the tow-truck operators tow you even if all you need is a jump start."

"Well, I'm not here to make a fortune off your *mis*fortune," she said, putting her glasses back on before she hopped down off the truck again. Her hands were trembling. Walking back to the tow bar, she added, "If I can fix whatever's wrong on the side of the road, I do it.

I believe in treating other people the way I'd like to be treated. And, to be honest, it saves me a lot of time too."

He was willfully wasting her time, but soon she'd have enough money to waste all the time she wanted.

"Well, you sure don't hear that philosophy much anymore," he said, watching her, amazed that she could make even the lowliest movement look agile—elegant even.

She laughed. "I hear it all the time. I borrowed it from my dad."

He thought of his own father—whose credo was to do unto others before they did unto you—and missed him. Not because of the way his dad thought or what he did, but maybe because he hadn't known any different. At least, that's what Noah wanted to believe. Had to believe. Needed to believe . . .

"So, Mr. Thomas," she said, breaking in on his thoughts, releasing the hydraulic hoist that lowered the tow bar to the ground as she wiggled her fingers into heavy work gloves. "What's a nice man like you doing in a place like this?"

"A little bit of everything," he said, smiling at the role reversal. "A little sightseeing. A little personal business. A little . . . business-business."

"What kind of business-business are you in?" She squatted, then got down on hands and knees to look under the car.

He'd known she would eventually ask the question, and he was prepared with an honest, if somewhat oblique answer.

"I'm with the government. They send me places to

look at things, make evaluations, write reports. Sometimes I implement changes. That's what I like to do, roll up my sleeves and make things change."

"What sort of things?" Maybe if she kept him talking he wouldn't notice what she was doing. She wasn't in the habit of wishing things different, but this once it would be nice to have a more ladylike job.

She tossed the heavy tow bar under the car as if it were a coat hanger. Noah took a second look at the muscles in her arms. She was a lot stronger than she looked.

"Ah . . . well, sometimes I work with mining companies to get them to try different mining techniques or introduce farmers to new farming methods, things like that." She had one side of the tow bar hooked to the front axle and was struggling with the other. "Can I help you with that?"

"No sense in both of us getting dirty," she said, her voice strained with a final effort to tip the hook over the metal bar. "There, got it." Her hands went directly to the next task of chaining the bar and wheels securely in place. "But thanks for the offer."

People who knew her rarely offered to help her with anything physical because they assumed she could handle it herself. Strangers generally went in three directions. Either they refused to offer help because they were paying for the service or they didn't offer to help because they were hoping to see her fail or they insisted on helping, assuming her gender required it. She liked that he held his offer until she looked as if she needed it.

"Have you been doing this long?" he asked, motioning to the truck.

"All my life," she said, getting to her feet. "My earliest memories are of going out with my dad. *This* was my job." She picked up a red plastic light and began to unwind the wires already attached to the taillights of the truck, slowly walking to the back of the car to attach it to the lid of trunk. "It's the most important job, you know," she said, repeating words she'd heard a hundred times. "Because it can save the lives of the people driving behind us, so they know this car is being towed, and no one's in it to control it."

Noah smiled at the simple logic that had been used to make her feel important as a child. For an instant something close to envy, coursed through him. He was eager to meet this man she called Dad, this man for whom his brother had given up his own father.

TWO

She didn't mind that he followed her up and down the length of the car talking to her while she worked, or that he was watching her as if her every movement fascinated him. What bothered her was that she was intensely aware of it—of him and the sound of his voice, the way he walked, and that he kept his hands in his pockets as if he couldn't trust them.

She was a minor authority on hands. The shape, the size, the character of them. Had been for a long time. She liked his hands. They were big, according to her mental measure, and shaped perfectly, as if a sculptor had spent many loving hours forming them. Slender. Graceful. And yet they were work-worn. Callused and peppered with small scars, they were hands that knew hard labor, the hands of an honest man.

A strange man, too, if the unconscious battle he was fighting with his clothes was any indication. She hadn't seen expensive, monogrammed shirts worn with the sleeves rolled up to the elbows before. He'd slipped his hands inside the collar to rub the places on his neck where the collar itched; unbuttoned another button every five minutes; finally pulled the tail of the shirt out of his pants to let it hang loose and damp in the arid air. He was much more comfortable and relaxed since he'd taken it off altogether, rolled it into a ball, and tossed it onto the backseat of the Escort. Seemed to her that if he preferred soft casual T-shirts to starched oxford button-downs, that's what he should have worn.

"So I didn't really make any appointments or tell anyone when I'd be in town," he was ad-libbing. "I figured that since I'd never been to this part of the country before, I'd just take my time and get a good look at it."

She gave the hoist one final back-and-forth jerk to make sure it, the safety chains, and the front end of the car were stable and secure, then asked, "Have you seen enough of this particular part of the country yet? Or would you like to take a few pictures before we go?"

"No no, I've seen plenty." He laughed. "More than enough. Take me away from this place." He was already climbing into the truck, pushing the cooler over between them. "I need food. I need an air-conditioned hotel room. I need a shower . . . and maybe a nap."

She chuckled, even as she noticed how incredibly small the cab of truck seemed all of a sudden. He was leaning on the door with his elbow out the window, but it felt as if he were sitting too close to her, rubbing against her, touching her, in spite of the two feet between them.

"Okay, Mr. Thomas, hang on, then. I'll get you

back to Gypsum in record time," she said, turning the key in the ignition.

If she called him Mr. Thomas again he'd scream, pull out his hair, and make a complete confession. It was like electric-shock torture, frying his nerves to a crisp.

There hadn't been another vehicle on the road since he'd pulled his over, but she still looked behind them before pulling onto the road and making a U-turn. Her long legs weren't simply objects of beauty, he noted appreciatively, they worked the clutch and brakes of the truck with ease; her arms maneuvered it as if it were a Matchbox toy.

"By the way, I'm Mich Albee," she said.

"Mich?" he said, pronouncing it as she had, with a *sh* at the end. This was the perfect time to ask her to call him Noah, but he just couldn't risk it yet.

A faint smile. "It's a long, dumb story. Michelin is my real name."

"It's pretty. Michelin," he said, enjoying the sound of it.

She slipped him an if-you-say-so look. She'd argued the merits of having an unusual name before, but win or lose, she was stuck with it.

For a few minutes they drove along in a comfortable silence, content to know everything was going as planned. But then the silence started to become uncomfortable. Should she say something? What could he ask her?

"Are there—"

"Where are you—"

They started speaking at once, then laughed when they realized they'd been thinking the same thing.

"Where are you from, Mr. Thomas?" she asked, flashing him a quick smile, wondering if she looked as jumpy as she felt. Something in her mind was ticking off every breath he took, knew his fingers were tapping lightly on the door, in time with a snappy country-western tune she could barely hear on the radio.

"Chicago originally. But like I said, I travel a lot—or I did, until recently. I have a small apartment in Washington, D.C., for when I'm between jobs."

"My husband was from Chicago," she said. "I don't think he liked it very much."

"Why not?" Looking interested was no pretense.

"Well, I think there were a lot of reasons why he wasn't happy there, but I think he just preferred wide-open spaces, fewer people."

"Lots of people get claustrophobic in big cities. But this"—he motioned to the harsh desert wasteland—"this is sort of extreme, don't you think?"

She laughed. "If you knew him, you wouldn't think so. I used to think Extreme was his middle name."

That her memories of his brother were fond was very clear, painfully so, in a way that made him happy and sad at the same time. She wasn't speaking as if he were alive and well and waiting for her in Gypsum, but she hadn't explained that he'd died either.

"Does he still have family in Chicago?" he couldn't help asking, couldn't believe it was going to be so easy to get information from her.

"His father still lives there, I think, and he has a brother somewhere."

"Is that right?" It was all he could do to manage a

mild, casual interest in his expression. "Does he get back to see them often?"

"Oh. No," she said quickly. "My husband's gone. Passed away. A long time ago."

"I'm sorry."

"Me too," she said wistfully. "I miss him." She hesitated then added, "It's strange, though. . . . I haven't talked about him in a long time."

"I'm sorry. I didn't mean to . . ."

"No, no. It's okay. I don't mind talking about him, I just . . . haven't in a while." She gave him an unreadable look. "You're easy to talk to."

"Well, thank you." His job was to listen to other people's problems, complaints, and concerns, to listen carefully and work out reasonable solutions. "I'm going to take that as a compliment."

"Do. I meant it as one."

They smiled at each other for a second or two, then quickly looked away.

Was he actually flirting with her? she wondered.

Was she liking him as much as he liked her? he hoped.

He wanted to know the whole story. All about her. How she and his brother met. About Eric's death. What her life had been like since then. All about the boy. He wanted to tell her who he really was and why he'd come, but he wasn't sure of the reception he'd get.

"How did your husband die? If you don't mind my asking."

She shrugged. "In a motorcycle accident."

Speeding down this very highway? Heart free, wind in his hair? With no responsibilities, an underdeveloped sense of duty, and a staunch passion to live? The pain of it twisted inside him.

"How long ago?"

"Almost fifteen years." She frowned. "Doesn't seem that long." She recalculated it in her head. Yes. Fifteen years. "That's strange."

"What?"

"That it's been so long."

"You must have a very good life if time is passing so quickly for you."

"A good life?" she repeated absently, glancing at him. It wasn't hard to recall how desperate she'd once been to get away from Gypsum, to dance in crowds of happy people, sleep in exotic places, see the world. But it was easier to remember why she'd given up those dreams, and she smiled. "Yeah. I guess I do have a pretty good life," she said, her expression softening with a whimsical smile. "It's not the one I set out to have, but it hasn't been bad. It could be a lot worse."

"In what way?" He crossed his arms and angled himself to see her better.

This time when she looked across the seat at him, her open expression was cautious and pensive, even with the dark glasses.

"Well, no matter how bad you think your life is, can't you always find someone else whose life is worse?"

"I guess so," he said, pondering her Pollyanna attitude. Did she apply it to everything or just this specific subject? At this specific time? He sensed it was an evasive maneuver and let her take it for now. "So, what sort of life did you set out to have?"

She laughed and looked at him.

"You ask a lot of questions," she said, unoffended, merely stating the fact.

"I know. I'm sorry," he said, not meaning it at all. "Habit, I guess. I like people. I like knowing about them."

She smiled, nodded, and accepted this without an objection, as if she understood his interest. Yet several minutes went by before she spoke again.

"I guess I wanted what everyone wants when they're young. Freedom. Excitement. Everything. All at once." She spoke softly, as if her view down the road went back in time. "But then I suppose I just assumed that once you'd seen everything and done everything, your life would automatically settle into some little house somewhere, with grass in the front yard and a swing set in back and . . . some man would come home every night and be glad and grateful to find you waiting for him. . . . Because I wanted that too. But . . . but not until I'd had the other. Not until I'd done it all." There was a long silence, and then her voice was even softer, lower. "You should have seen him the first day he showed up in Gypsum on that Harley," she said, and Noah knew she was talking about his brother, Eric— then just five years older than his son was now. "He was excitement on wheels. It was like . . . he walked around inside a cloud of electricity, a storm cloud, and everywhere he went the air would sizzle and snap with his energy. He'd walk into a room and the lights would dim, flicker off and on, and you knew, you just knew . . ."

Her words trailed off and she seemed to catch herself; to hear her own words in the air, and she laughed suddenly.

"Who *are* you?" she asked, looking quizzical. It startled him. "Are you sure we haven't met before? I feel like I must know you from somewhere." She flipped her cap off onto the seat and shook her hair out with her fingers. "I can't believe I'm telling you all this stuff."

He couldn't either.

"I'm easy to talk to, remember?" he said, making light of it to ease her chagrin. His brow furrowed when he realized how much he wanted to run his fingers through her hair too. It brushed the top of her shoulders, thick, dark, and shiny. He imagined it would feel cool and smooth sliding between his fingers.

She nodded and laughed softly at herself, but kept her mouth firmly closed. She never shared her memories of Eric, except sometimes with her son. She hoarded her memories, nurtured them, lived them again and again in the middle of the night when loneliness was her best and only lover. What had possessed her to waste even a drop of their vitality on this man? This . . . this very strange stranger.

One more time they smiled at each other, both completely aware that their relationship, however brief, transcended the businesslike nature of its start.

The trip back to Gypsum seemed much shorter than the fifty miles he'd driven earlier to launch his infiltration into his brother's family. Michelin absently picked up a hand grip from the seat beside her and began to squeeze it slowly, rhythmically, barely rippling the smooth muscles of her forearm as she talked. She told him that the Mormons had come to settle the desert first, battling off the Paiute Indians. Finally, she offered to loan him a truck and told him he might like to visit the small Duckwater Indian Reservation to the north or the Lunar Crater to the south, and that the White Pine Mountains were nice, too, but not another word of a personal nature did she utter.

Gypsum wasn't even on U.S. Highway 6. Small yellow signs marked its existence coming and going, and the only other acknowledgment it got from the government was two paved ramps leading off and on the highway, going to and from the hard-packed dirt roads that became Gypsum's main street a mile and a half to the southeast.

"Saloon?" he said, reading the rudimentary sign on the small building as they passed it. He'd wondered about it earlier. It was an old-fashioned word, even for a run-down old-fashioned town.

"Yep," she said, grinning. "And there's the General Store. The Bank. The Jail. The Hotel. The Bath House," she said, calling out the labels on each establishment as they passed it. "But that's actually a clothing store now, and Willa keeps a couple coin-operated washers and dryers in the back." She pointed a finger to his side of the street. "There's the other saloon, but it's not really a saloon. The town's not big enough to support two, so Hank Meally has a few antiques and souvenirs and . . . tourist junk in there. It's the Chamber of Commerce, too, so we call it the Other Saloon so we don't get them mixed up."

She laughed at the expression on his face. "Bet you didn't know Gypsum was a famous town, did you?"

"Famous for what?"

"Well," she said haughtily, "John Wayne made two movies here. One in the early sixties and then another in the early seventies. The first time, they came in and rebuilt all the storefronts, put in all the porches and walks and railings . . . and the signs. And when they came back the second time, they repainted everything so you could make out the signs on camera. It was a real boon for us. That second coat of paint is pretty much the only thing holding this place together."

"And now you're waiting for the great revival of western movies," he said, not guessing.

"Yep. The town council says why mess with a good thing when you've got it? We'll just sit here looking like a ghost town till somebody needs one."

There was a tone of affectionate sarcasm in her voice, directed at herself as much as the town. A gentle mocking of something she loved.

"How many people live here?" he asked.

"Exactly thirty. Two years ago there were forty-five, but people die here faster than we can replace them. But all totaled, there's almost two hundred citizens in the general area. I'm the official census keeper, by the way."

"A fellow government employee," he said, teasing her.

She snapped her fingers and pointed one at him. "I bet that's where I know you from, the company picnic."

"Very likely," he said, not wanting to pursue this feeling she had of knowing him from somewhere.

"Poor Dad, of course, wasn't in on the movie deals. They offered to turn the front of the gas station into a smithy and build stables and a corral around it, but he was thinking long-term in those days," she said, driving head-on into the Albee Trucking company yard. A cloud of dust surrounded them. "He was convinced no one would stop at a livery stable for gas, and he was just getting into the trucking business then and knew he'd be needing the bigger shop."

She motioned with her head toward a hugh blue-and-white aluminum structure perhaps two hundred yards off the main road and far to the side of the smaller, older building that was the gas station and auto repair shop he'd stopped at that morning.

There was a collection of vehicles in varying degrees of disintegration parked beside and behind the station, and she eased the tow truck to a stop in the middle of them.

He was trying very hard not to make any judgments about the place, but . . . it was a dump. Old, run-down, falling apart, rusty, dirty, neglected. There was an old bicycle leaning against the building and a big golden-colored dog asleep under the only window in front. He wondered about his nephew, what his life was like here, what he was like, what his expectations were and his dreams.

"I know what you're thinking," she said. He could feel the blood draining out of his face as he turned to look at her. "You're thinking he should have taken the movie deal." She laughed. "Well, you're right. He should have. I tell him all the time that tourists would recognize the gas pumps and stop, even if it did have 'blacksmith' over the door. But no," she said, opening the door and getting out. "He won't even consider it."

Noah got out then, too, wondering if the nervous-ness he'd felt earlier had caused him to miss the deplorable conditions of this place when he'd seen it the first time. Even the dog was too old and feeble to do more than lift a brow and an eyelid to indicate his interest in a stranger.

"And we could have used the corral," she said, coming around the truck. "Eric wasn't here then, of course, but we keep a couple of horses now, and we had to build stables and a corral back at the house for them."

Of course, he thought, relieved. They didn't *live* here. There was a house someplace. He watched her walk to the open front door of the station and call for her son. A house with curtains and perhaps not grass, as she'd dreamed, but a swing set in the backyard wouldn't be out of order. . . .

"Eric?" she called again, then pulled back when a boy rounded the corner of the building.

Noah's breath stuck in his throat; his heart skipped a beat, then another. The waves of heat blurred his sight and distorted time. It was Eric, taller perhaps than what he remembered, but the similarities were so . . . so similar, it was all he could do to keep from calling out to him.

"Hi," he told his mother, spinning a basketball on the end of his index finger. He wore jeans, T-shirt, and sneakers; his hair was cut short and uncombed. "That didn't take you long." He caught the ball in both hands and leaned a little sideways to get a good look at Noah. "Hi."

"Hi." The word came out breathlessly. He swallowed hard, then took several steps forward. "How's it going?"

"Okay," Eric said, with much the same keen, evaluating stare his mother had.

I'm your uncle and I've come to give you everything you've ever dreamed of, he wanted to say, but instead he simply nodded.

"Eric, this is Mr. Thomas. He's going to need a room down at the Hotel, and he's hungry. Will you walk him down and make sure he gets settled?"

"Sure," the boy said, giving a sort of whole-body shrug indicating he had nothing better to do. "Granddad said to tell you he tried both Charlie's place and Lou Garrett's, and they're both waiting for replacement parts too." He tossed the basketball around the corner of the building toward the back and went on, "He tried that guy in Ely too. He had one but wouldn't let us have it, in case he needed it. And Frank won't be coming through here for three more days, but he said he could express us a new belt if we wanted to pay the charges."

They both looked at Noah.

"Oh, ah, no. That won't be necessary," he said, caught off guard, amazed by how much Eric's voice sounded like his brother's at that age. "Like I said, I'm in no hurry and . . . and here I am in an authentic western-movie town." He held out both hands as if he could ask for nothing more.

Michelin smiled and the boy shook his head, bewildered. After all, once seen, who'd *want* to stay in Gypsum, Nevada? Other than it's thirty inhabitants and his own brother, of course?

Mother and son walked together toward him and the tow truck, almost equal in height, possibly in weight as well. They were comfortable with each other, he noticed with definite envy.

"I was telling Mr. Thomas about the horses. He might like to see them later."

"Okay," Eric said, not seeming to mind that he'd just been volunteered to show them. "Can you ride?"

"It's been a while," Noah said, watching Michelin walk around to the other side of the truck, preparing to lower and disconnect the Escort. He turned back to Eric. "I'd like to try it again. But I don't want to put you to any trouble."

Up close he could see that the boy had his mother's dark eyes, deep brown with golden flecks. But his lazy, good-natured smile belonged to his father.

"No trouble. You can actually see 'em from here, on the way to the Hotel."

"You can?"

"Yeah, they're just back there," he said, pointing in some vague direction beyond the gas station. "You got a suitcase or something?"

"Ah, yes," he said, turning quickly to the Escort, opening th back door to remove his duffel bag and dirty shirt. He was prepared for anything that came his way, right? He had to remind himself. "Oh. It's alive," he said, turning back to see that the big golden dog, a wiry-haired creature with a terrier face, had roused himself to come stand beside the boy. "I thought he was a rug at first."

This amused Eric and he laughed out loud.

"His name's Lugnut. We call him Lug for short."

"How old is he?" Noah asked, grasping at the boy's obvious fondness for the animal.

"Ninety-one," he said, then added, "In dog years. In people years he's only thirteen. A year younger than me."

Eric turned to lead the way down the dusty street—Lug and Noah followed him. He measured the boy's height to be just above his shoulder and felt completely connected to him in some invisible, unjustified, extremely complicated manner that he wouldn't try to comprehend just then. It was enough simply to walk beside him, hear him, study him. He felt as if he'd traveled the earth searching for him.

"See there," the boy said, pointing. "The bay is mine and"—he raised his voice—"that old brown nag belongs to Mom."

"I heard that," Mich shouted, and when Noah turned his head to look back at her, she was smiling, with one hand propped on her hip. "And I've had that old nag almost as long as I've had you, buster. Show a little respect."

Eric walked backward, grinning mischievously at her. When they both turned away, he picked up where he'd left off. "Butch is back there, too, somewhere. He's pretty gentle. Won't give you any trouble."

"Oh, I don't want to put anyone out," Noah said, craning his neck to get a better look at the house. It was a square, single-story building with a door and two windows on either side, that might have once been white but now shown silver gray in the bright sun. It stood alone and detached from the rest of the town and the buildings belonging to the trucking company—without adornment or landscaping. No swing set in sight.

"She won't care if you ride," the boy said, sounding

sure of this. "Or she wouldn't have volunteered me to show them to you."

"Oh."

Eric grinned. "She volunteers me for everything," he said. He hesitated, glancing briefly at Noah. "Especially if she thinks I'll learn something from it."

"And what does she think you'll learn from me, I wonder?"

"Beats me," he said honestly. "The meaning of a word I don't know yet. About the place you come from. Another way to tie my shoes—I never know. But she says I can learn something from everyone I meet, and since there's never anyone new here, she looks for opportunities for me." They exchanged blank stares. "I know," he went on with a short laugh. "She's weird that way."

"Well . . . maybe it isn't so weird," Noah said, giving her the benefit of the doubt. "You can learn a lot from other people."

He thought of his experiences in the mines with the natives of Angola and Tanzania; of the eighteen months he spent in the wilds of Zaire; of the philosophy of life he'd heard from a Muslim in Al-Hamma that had made so much sense to him, he'd adopted it as his own.

"I pretty much know all I want to know right now," the boy said with the all-knowing certitude of teenagers —not bothering to look both ways before crossing the street. "But she's got this thing about me growing up to be an educated man. It's dumb."

"Why is it dumb?"

Eric screwed his face up thoughtfully. "Well *it's* not dumb, just the reason she wants it is dumb."

"Oh," Noah said, and would have gone on to ask what her reasons were—was eager to in fact—but they'd come to a stop in front of the building marked HOTEL.

"This isn't really a hotel, you know," Eric said, as if to warn him. "Greta Mathews lives here and she rents out rooms. Two of 'em. She's nice but . . . well, she drinks a little sometimes. If that's not okay, you could probably stay at our house, only one of my uncles is home now."

"No," Noah said definitely, absolutely not ready to move in with the family. "Thanks, but I've been known to drink a little sometimes too. Greta and I will get along fine, I'm sure."

"Don't go to the Bank 'cuz that's just a fake front. If you need to cash a check or something, you can do it at the General Store or the Saloon. And you don't have to worry about going to jail while you're here, 'cuz that's not really there either."

"I see. So . . . if I were a bank robber, that would be the good news and the bad news, huh?"

The boy grinned and laughed. "Yeah," he said, giving Noah a friendly, appreciative glance that warmed his heart. "I guess it would be."

Eric knocked on the Hotel door as he opened it and stuck his head inside shouting, "Hey! Greta, you here?" There was no sound in response. He opened the door farther and walked in, saying, "Come on in."

Eric walked around in the space that was more foyer than lobby, poking his head into one room after another until he found what he was looking for.

Noah followed to the door he disappeared through and watched the boy cover a small gray-haired woman with a brighly colored afghan. He removed a near-empty shot glass from her fingertips, set it beside the gin bottle on the coffee table, screwed the top on the bottle, then snuck out of the room.

"She's sleeping," he whispered to Noah, though they both knew she was fried to the gills. "I'll leave her a note that you're here, and you can go on up to the room. She charges six bucks a night and feeds you breakfast if she's awake." He shrugged. "If she isn't, you can go next door to the Saloon. They got lunch and supper, too, if you want. Or you can go on down the street to Eddy's Diner. He's got the chicken special going on down there this week. Just remember, cold food at the Saloon, hot food at Eddy's. That's how it works here."

He opened a drawer in a small table next to the front door, took out a key, and gave it to Noah—who stood watching him with his mouth open. "You can use this if you feel like locking the door. It goes to the room at the top of the stairs, on the right. It has a telephone and a TV, but you can only get two channels here. . . . But if you want to see something special on TV, you can come to our house, we got a satellite dish three years ago. And the bathroom is . . . what?"

"What?"

"You're staring at me funny."

"Oh. Sorry. You just seem so . . . used to doing this," Noah said, trying to take it all in, get a clear picture of the boy's life thus far.

"I *am* used to it. We help each other out around here. I can do lots of things."

Noah nodded. as if he understood.

"Most boys your age would be uncomfortable dealing with adults. Helping them out. Talking with them. Showing them around. They'd want to be off with their pals, doing something fun."

"Well, little kids and old people are about all I know," the boy said, seeming to think nothing of Noah's observations as he took a pen and paper from the drawer and starting to write. "Me and Corie Wilks are the only in-betweens. Not little kids anymore. Not old, either."

"A girl?"

"Well, nobody's too sure about that yet. We're all waitin' to see," he said, repugnance in his voice.

"Then who do you talk to? Who are your friends?" Noah asked, concerned now about his nephew's social development too.

"I talk to everyone. They're all my friends," he answered, looking puzzled.

"What about school? Don't you have friends at school?"

A cloud covered the boy's features, rousing emotions in the depths of his eyes that were difficult to read.

"I don't go to school," he said, returning to his note to Greta. Then, with a mix of pride and determination in his voice, he added, "Never have, never will."

THREE

Something was terribly wrong.

Noah sat down on the edge of the bed in the small, but neat and clean, room of the Hotel. He'd put away what few belongings he'd brought with him, but needed time to collect his thoughts.

The boy had never been to school. How could this be? Though he could read and write and spoke well, if not better than most boys his age, he needed to know more of the world than Gypsum, Nevada.

What could she be thinking? His mind drifted back to Michelin Albee. Thick dark hair, long long legs. Those deep dark eyes . . . He stirred uncomfortably.

She obviously loved her son and had his best interests at heart. He remembered the way her face lit up when she talked about him, how animated she was when she was with him. She wasn't an ignorant, backward woman. She knew the boy needed an education. . . .

All right, he was broad-minded enough to know there was a difference between going to school and getting an education—a vast distinction. But then, what about peer pressure, girls, competitive sports? Those were things a boy his age needed to experience, needed to know about. What about his future? What about career opportunities?

Well, that was why he'd come, wasn't it? To meet Michelin Albee, get to know his nephew, make sure they were both well provided for, help them in any way he could.

He hadn't come to upset any applecarts, certainly had very little right to after all this time—but more and more he was beginning to feel there was a certain responsibility innate to unclehood.

If the boy was not being treated kindly or brought up properly, was not being educated or given at least the advantages an average American boy should get, well then, didn't Noah owe it to his brother to step in? Wouldn't that be his duty as an uncle?

He sighed aloud in the unavailing silence. What did he know about raising kids? Aside from the fact that he'd been one once . . . and hadn't *that* been a fiasco? The finest schools, the best of friends, every door pushed wide open to him, and yet he'd never been happy. Eric either. He gathered up his shaving gear and went out into the hallway looking for a shower.

Perhaps it was too early to make any judgments. There could be a reason Michelin hadn't sent the boy to school, though for the life of him he couldn't think of what it might be. He found the linen closet where Eric said it would be and removed a towel, opening the next door to the bathroom. He hated to entertain the thought, but he knew he could "outlawyer" her in a custody suit—take the boy from this godforsaken town and show him the world.

He shucked his damp, dirty clothes into a pile in the middle of the floor. He could give the boy everything. Take him back to Chicago or even Washington. He frowned, thinking of Michelin once again. Well, she could come, too, he supposed.

He let the tepid water rain on his head and run down his back, sighing once more with indecision. It was possible that a court battle wouldn't be necessary. They'd probably be grateful for his help, welcome it if he was careful in choosing his moment to offer it. Hadn't the boy said that his mother wanted him to be an educated man? She seemed a sensible woman, perhaps she'd readily admit that the best she could give her son wasn't good enough.

And what about his own life?

Caring for his brother's wife and son would definitely put a crimp in his own lifestyle. He might have to cut back on his overseas assignments. If he set them up in their own residence, his life between assignments could go on without much change. . . .

He held the bar of soap against his chest and strained to listen.

"Yes?" he called to the second set of loud raps at the bathroom door, thinking it a particularly uncomfortable moment for his landlady to stumble up the steps to make his acquaintance.

"Walt Albee here," came a deep rumbling voice through the door. "The girl sent me over to tell you to join us at Eddy's when you're ready to eat supper. She says it's lonely to eat alone in a strange place."

Walt was the grandfather, Michelin's father, he knew from the investigator's report he'd acquired a few short weeks ago. Twice widowed, he had no criminal record, no outstanding debts, and few vices. Someone his brother had labeled "a good man."

"That's very kind of her, Mr. Albee," he said, turning off the water and grabbing the towel. "Please tell her I'll be down shortly and I'd . . ."

His voice trailed off as he opened the door, standing in a puddle of water, knotting the towel at his waist, to find no one there. He peeked out into the hall. Empty.

Apparently no reply was required. Apparently it hadn't been an invitation as much as a directive. Apparently he'd be dining with Michelin Albee whether he wanted to or not.

Okay. So he wanted to. It was still an uncommon manner of invitation that left him feeling defensive when he walked into Eddy's Diner nearly an hour later, not wanting to appear too . . . easy. You see, it was he who generally set the sequence of events. It was his job to find the problems and take the steps required to solve them. He was used to running every—

The diner was empty.

Eddy's was located on the north end of town, closest to the highway and well away from the more historical-looking buildings—with plenty of parking space for the buses that passed through on a twenty-four-hour schedule. A small establishment by most standards, the place boasted ten booths, five on each wall, and five more tables on the floor in between. And they were all empty. There was a lunch counter at the back, a kitchen beyond that, and except for the man in a sagging white chef's hat leaning on his fist in the window looking out, not a soul was there.

"Your name Thomas?" the man asked after a second or two, dropping his arm on the counter to appear almost interested.

"Yes," Noah said. He'd now lied about his name to five people either directly or indirectly—the number was becoming oppressive. "I was supposed to meet—"

"Yeah, yeah . . . the girl was here already. Told me to tell ya she'd be back about five-thirty. Buck brought his rig back with a skip in the transmission or somethin'. Has to fix it tonight 'cuz he's got another run in the mornin', but she and the boy need to eat sometime, she said, so they'll be here at five-thirty. If you don't mind waitin'," he added, as if instructed to. "Told me to introduce myself. The name's Maximilian Bayan. They call me Max. This is my place."

"How do you do, Max," Noah said, taking a seat at the counter to wait for his dinner companions. Then, as it occurred to him, he asked, "Isn't this Eddy's place?"

Max grinned then, displaying a broad rakish smile and the fact that most his teeth were set sideways.

"Nah. Before I stumbled onto this place it was John Rumpski's place and before that a man named Lester Degress had it. Eddy Phipps had the place built and slapped his name up on the windows and then died of heatstroke before the grand openin'. The place was closed for two years before they had their first customer." He put a toothpick in his mouth and talked around it. "They say it's bad luck. The second owner, Lester Degress, tangled with a sidewinder right out back here. Kilt him dead. The fellah before me, John

Rumpski—hell if his wife didn't shoot him in the ear one afternoon. Went clean through his head."

"You're not a superstitious man, I take it?" Noah joked.

"Nah," said Max, waving his hand in front of his face as if swatting at a fly. "I ain't married and I got two wooden legs, I got nothin' to worry about." Noah lowered his hands slowly to the countertop, staring at the man, not sure if he should laugh at his joke or sympathize with him. "You want somethin' to drink?" Max asked.

"I do," Eric said, having entered the diner unnoticed by Noah, who turned around to smile at him. "Can I have a soda?"

"Sure," Max said, his grin his greeting. Then he turned and walked away from the window, rocking slightly from side to side as if he might indeed have bilateral protheses. Over his shoulder he added, "Tend to Mr. Thomas, too, will ya?"

"What'll ya have?" Eric asked, from the other side of the lunch counter, slapping his palms flat on the top as if he were a bartender. It occurred to Noah that Eric was probably as comfortable behind the bar at the Saloon as he was behind the lunch counter at Eddy's and doling out rooms at the Hotel. "Want a menu?"

"Ah, no. I'll have what you're having."

Eric gathered glasses and ice. While filling them from the tap, he glanced twice over his shoulder to see if Max was within hearing range.

"Was Max telling you this place was bad luck?" he asked, leaning forward and speaking in a near whisper.

Noah nodded. "I'm wondering if it's safe to eat here."

Eric grinned and pulled away to finish filling the glasses. "Just for the record," he said, voice still low, "he only has one artificial leg. He lost it in Vietnam. And Eddy was his brother. Lost him there too."

"Oh," Noah said, torn between irritation at being lied to and empathy for the man's losses. Eric was walking toward a booth with both drinks. Noah followed him. "But then why—"

"Max says his version of the story is more interesting and takes longer to tell," he was already saying. He passed Noah a conspirator's grin. "He says the tourists love it. Especially the ladies. He picks the one with the most sympathy in her face and tells her that he really has one leg missing, and that he lost it trying to save his high-school sweetheart when their car got stuck on a railroad track one night. Train came, killed her, took his leg—it's from an old song or something. Then he says, when they pulled his sweetheart from the wreckage she had his high-school ring in her hand. Max says it tears them up. Can't keep their hands off him after that."

"I see." Noah lowered his gaze to his drink.

Instead of going to school, his nephew was being raised in a den of drunks, compulsive liars, and womanizers. He wondered if the attorney who lived on the floor above him in Washington could recommend a good Nevada lawyer?

"He doesn't mean anything by it," Eric said, seeing the disapproval in his face. "Max says if the tourists even bother to remember the story, it gives them something interesting to talk about when they get home—and he doesn't really do anything about the ladies. He just likes to talk big."

He studied Eric's features. He was so young. His innocence sparkled in his eyes, clear and bright. His expression was so open, devoid of painful memories, shocking experiences . . . there was no wariness there. He was like a sheet of snow-white paper, waiting to be written on.

And yet there was a wisdom in the way he tipped his head to one side when he was thinking, in the lowering of his gaze before he allowed himself to express his thoughts.

"You're very mature for your age, Eric," Noah said before he could stop himself. "Very accepting of other people's faults and foibles, their frailties."

The boy jerked a shoulder and looked away, self-conscious. "Nobody's perfect."

Now, that was a huge lesson most adults didn't know.

"You know, don't you, that you're being raised differently from most boys your age? In this tiny town. In the middle of nowhere. Not many kids your own age around . . ."

Eric looked at him then, his eyes narrowing slightly with . . . suspicion? An uncomfortable moment passed before he spoke.

"My mom says you work for the government."

"I do," Noah said, aware that the boy had deliberately changed the subject. "I'm with . . . the Diplomatic Corps," he said, barely hesitating. He waited, expecting the sky to fall on him. It was a risk to tell him at this point, but he wanted to be truthful with the boy.

"I go to foreign countries a lot. Meet with other governments' officials—"

"There's my mom," Eric said abruptly, almost as a warning.

Noah frowned, watching the boy watch his mother cross the street. If he'd said, *Don't tell her what you just told me,* it couldn't have been less surprising.

Slowly, wondering at the boy's sudden reticence, he turned his head to the door. Michelin Albee entered, and it was as if the entire diner filled with her scent, like a fresh gust of wind. Something about her—her spirit, her energy maybe—seemed too grand, too vast to fit inside four walls. Something about her commanded attention, demanded respect. He thought of the way Walt Albee and then again Max Bayan had referred to "the girl" earlier, and he'd automatically known it was she, instinctively knew that her biddings were preeminent to all.

And yet seeing her now, she seemed totally unaware of her power.

"Hi," she said, smiling, ridiculously glad that she'd taken the time to shower and change into clean jeans and smear a little lipstick on. It hadn't been three hours, but the man she'd been so anxious to see again was even more attractive than she'd remembered.

He looked so out of place in his pressed Dockers and polo shirt, so unlike the dusty jean-clad cowboy and trucker types who passed through. He looked like a picture in a magazine.

"Sorry I'm late," she said, nearing the table. "I'm sure Eric told you what a mess I was after—is something wrong?" she asked, looking from son to stranger.

"I forgot to tell him you'd be late." Eric's voice and manner were oddly dull and reserved.

"Oh," she said, still confused. That wasn't enough of an explanation for the tension she felt between them. "Well, I was covered in grease. My brother—"

"Please . . ." Noah held up a hand to stop her apology and realized he'd have waited a great deal longer just to see her again. "I appreciate you taking the time to make me feel at home here. I eat alone a lot. This is a real treat for me. Sit down, please."

She slid in beside Eric, who leaned sullenly against the wall, sneaking glances at Noah now and then.

"I don't suppose your room at the hotel is what you're used to—" she started, and was once again cut off.

"It's a fine room. Very adequate," he said, not wanting to talk small talk. Wanting instead to be candid with her, to ask her personal questions, to end this charade and take his proper place in her life.

And he would. Soon. As soon as he had all the information he needed, and as soon as the right moment presented itself. He hated deceiving her.

"In fact," he said, forcing an upbeat tone, "Gypsum is proving to be more . . . colorful than it first appeared."

"Oh?" She glanced briefly at Eric, wondering at his strange behavior. But then, what was stranger than the mood swings of a teenager? Or a full-grown man for that matter? She would have sworn he was tense and upset when she'd first walked in, but now . . . well, perhaps she'd been mistaken. "Colorful, huh? How so?"

"I've never eaten in a diner with such a history of bad luck. I keep waiting for the roof to fall in."

She laughed then. She could tell he'd heard Max's stories, and Eric's factual revisions, by his knowing expression.

"Oh yes. Very colorful, don't you think?" she asked. "You should be glad you're not going to be here that long. The line between fact and fiction is very thin here. You'd be amazed what heat and boredom can do to perfectly sane people."

"It doesn't seem to have affected you much. You're very direct and—"

"What's this? Still no food on the table?"

Noah was startled at the big voice that bounced off the walls and rattled the windows. He recognized it, though previously there had been a door between them to cushion its volume. The owner of the voice, a grizzly bear–size man who'd just entered the diner, lumbered toward them at an unstoppable pace.

"Here I thought I'd be late enough to just sit down and eat," Walt Albee exclaimed. "Max! What the hell you doin' back there? Cookin'?" He looked at Noah then. "Whole town knows his chicken special comes straight out of a box. How you doin'? We met earlier."

"I remember," Noah said, offering his hand, prepared to have it crushed. "Pleased to meet you, Mr. Albee."

"Walt," the older man said. He'd have to be split down the middle, and half of him sent to sit elsewhere, to fit comfortably into the booth with them. So he pulled a table from the middle of the room up to their booth, grabbed a chair along the way, and sat down.

"The girl tells me you had some trouble on the road. Strange, the belt goin' like that on a new car."

"Yes. That's what your daughter said." Looking at her made him feel safe and protected somehow. "And I'm definitely going to show that belt to someone when I return the car," he added quickly, wondering if his face was as red as it was hot. "They're lucky it was only the fan belt. There could be a serious malfunction in the engine."

"We'll give it a good once-over before you set out again, don't you worry about that."

"No no, I'm not worried. I was just thinking of the next people to rent that car. The company may even want to take it out of their rental fleet completely, just to be safe." Noah cringed inwardly; without a doubt, he was the world's *worst* liar. "On the other hand, it could have been just one of those things. . . ."

Why wasn't anyone stopping him?

"What's this? No food on the table yet?"

At the sound of two new booming voices, Noah vowed to sit facing the entrance if he ever ate at Eddy's again and turned to see two Scandinavian warriors dressed in denim and plaid flannel approaching them. His first instinct was to run for his life.

"Go see what the hell Max is doin' back there," Walt told the Vikings, barely glancing at them.

Noah had always felt himself to be "big enough" at six-two, but these two men dwarfed him, being inches taller and considerably heavier.

"Mr. Thomas, these are my brothers. Buck," she indicated the one pulling up another table and chair to the table adjoining the booth, while the other lumbered off to the kitchen—"and Otis. I have another brother, Roy, but he's not due back for several days."

She watched her father's and brothers' reactions carefully. They all tended to distrust outsiders, as did she, but it would be reassuring to know she wasn't the only one to feel whatever it was about this man that drew her to him and stirred such curious emotions inside her.

He said it was a pleasure to meet them and shook Buck's hand, all the while wondering if any of them had a violent temper. What would his face look like when they discovered that Thomas was his *middle* name? That the rest of the world knew him as Noah Thomas Tessler, roving ambassador affiliated with the U.S. State Department; son of William F. Tessler, who had refused to acknowledge his only grandson; brother of Eric Tessler, who had impregnated the daughter and sister of these hulking giants before him, but, if the marriage registry of Nevada was correct—and it appeared it was—didn't live long enough to marry her.

She sat across from him, quiet and thoughtful, her presence as imposing as her brothers', as if she were eight times her size and stronger than all of them somehow.

"Tell me, Walt, which came first? The family or the trucking company?" Noah asked, knowing people enjoyed talking about themselves.

Walt rumbled a laugh. "You mean did I have all the kids so they could drive truck for me or did I drive truck so I could feed 'em all?"

"Yes . . ." Noah chuckled along with them.

The art of diplomacy came naturally to him—most

of the time. That night it rubbed his nerves raw to ask all the right questions, give the proper responses, make himself appear reasonable and amiable and still maintain an outsider's objectivity. But then, he wasn't an outsider, was he? Eric was as much his nephew as theirs, and Michelin was . . .

Well no, his feelings toward her were anything but sisterly, he had to admit.

Over and over during the meal he caught himself watching her. He noted the sharp awareness in her eyes, the quick smile, the soft curve of her neck, the sureness of her hands, the lack of hesitation in offering an opinion or answering a question. And strangely enough, the undercurrent of silent communication between her and Eric—the way he'd somehow obtained permission to eat his chicken with his fingers, while she cut hers from the bone, the manner in which she stopped him from licking his fingers with a single glance.

It wasn't just Noah reacting to her invisible power. They all were—father, brothers, and son. Their behavior, however, was explained by a respect that had developed over the years, a knowledge of her capabilities.

His own fascination with her was as mindless and unerring as a heat-seeking missile. He just plain wanted to get close to her. To touch her. To know her. All of her . . .

Mich laid her fork and knife across her plate, the size of the knot in her stomach keeping her from eating her typically hardy helpings of Max's chicken special that evening.

He wanted her, this Mr. N. Thomas, this mysterious stranger, this charmer of fathers and brothers who conjured something more than friendliness in her. She knew men better than she knew herself sometimes. She could tell. This man wanted her. Oh, he was Mr. Casual Politeness in manner and phrase, but in his eyes he was come-sit-on-my-lap-baby through and through.

She glanced at him, caught him staring again, and didn't look away. Knowing she intrigued him made her want to giggle, made her skin tingle. There wasn't anything wrong with it. God knew she'd put up with enough ogling and panting in her time to be entitled to a light flirtation now and again. There wasn't anything wrong with a man and a woman liking each other and enjoying it, was there?

But, like the vast majority of her encounters with men, this one would be short-lived. Her life being what it was, she met men in bars, at truck stops, and occasionally along the side of the road. She was one of those ships that passed in the night. That old cliché was her life.

And despite the fact that she'd been sorely tempted more than once, she found it difficult to be a one-night stand with men she didn't know well . . . which wasn't to say that one or two men hadn't gotten to know her *very* well or that she'd been celibate for fifteen years.

After all, a woman had needs now and again. Like now, as she looked across the table at a darkly handsome man with eyes the color of the stormy green seas she'd only read about, with a certain come-to-me expression she'd dreamed of so often. . . .

"That's amazing," he said, pulling her attention back to the table. He was smiling over at Eric with great interest. "So you're a computer freak. That's great."

The boy shrugged. "Not really. I use it for my lessons mostly. And there's a bookkeeping program for small businesses. Taxes too. Granddad could have done it himself. Just had to read the directions," he said, peevish. "Can I be excused now? I got stuff to do."

"Sure." Mich frowned at his behavior. Unlike her father and brothers, her son was being uniquely unfriendly to their guest. "Don't forget to check the horses, please."

"I won't," Eric said, waiting for her to move so he could escape. He met Noah's gaze straight on for the first time in an hour. There was no emotion, positive or negative, to be deciphered. He slid out of the booth and walked out into the street, where Lugnut waited for him.

"Well," Noah said in the uncomfortable silence that followed. "I guess I blew my chance to at least *sound* mechanical. I don't know a carburetor from a piston, but I do know what downloading and hard drives are."

"Ha! You mean downshifting and overdrive," Otis said from his own table, third from the booth, missing the point completely and guffawing heartily. The rest of them merely smiled. It had become clear during the meal that Otis wasn't the sharpest tack on the wall, but of the three Albee men still present he was the most outgoing. "Well, don't you worry about the boy. He don't care what you know. He's as right as they come, most the time. Him and his mom are havin' a . . . ah . . . what'd you call it, Mich?"

"A difference of opinion," she said helpfully, knowing intuitively that it wasn't the cause of her son's present funk.

"Yeah," Buck chimed in. "She's of the opinion he needs to be sent away to school, and he's of the opinion that he just plain ain't goin'."

"Come about August we'll be seein' some real fireworks around here," Walt said with a constrained look at his daughter. "Never knew two people more stubborn than the two of them. Be real interesting to see who wins this one."

"We'll both win this time," she said, although she could have said *I'll have my way* with a lot less air. "However, I don't feel like discussing it right now, Dad. I have a transmission to put back together," she said, making it sound as easy as composing E-mail. She stood beside the booth ready to leave, then glanced at Noah. "It wouldn't take much to talk these guys into taking you down to the Saloon for a couple beers and some music. I'm afraid that's about all the nightlife Gypsum has to offer."

"No, no, that's fine. Tomorrow night I'll buy for anyone I can talk into coming with me. But I think I'll turn in early tonight. It's been a long day for me."

"Nothing tires you more than having things go wrong," Walt said, shaking his big gray head. He then addressed himself to Mich. "How's the arm today?"

"Hammer hard," she said, grinning and flexing her right arm for him.

"Good, girl. You best walk Mr. Thomas back to the Hotel, Mich. Stick your head inside and make sure Greta ain't smokin' one of those little see-gars she likes so much. Can't have her burning the place down around him, now can we?"

Noah's wide-eyed look of alarm had them all laughing, but no one bothered to negate Walt's words.

And so it was with a definite sense of uneasiness that he thanked them for their company and bid them good night before he followed Michelin out the door.

"You have a nice family," he said after walking beside her for several minutes in silence. The setting sun had turned the horizon a golden russet color, outlining distant land formations barely noticeable in the heat of the day. It was truly beautiful . . . but then so was the woman beside him. "Thank you. For tonight. For sharing them with me."

"I think they enjoyed you." She was looking straight ahead, walking slowly. There were definite drawbacks to living in a town you could traverse on foot, end to end, in less than five minutes. "It's nice to have someone different to talk to sometimes."

"You think I'm different?"

"Than what we're used to, yes. Most people who pass through here want to talk about themselves. Tell us who they are, where they're from, where they're going, as if they feel sorry for us because they're mobile and we're . . . fixed objects who've never seen or done anything outside this town." She paused. "You have a way of drawing people out."

What could he say? It was both a gift and a talent he worked at.

"And saying very little about yourself," she added.

"Well, why would I want to draw myself out? I already know all about me."

She smiled at his verbal two-step. "But the rest of us

don't. And some of us would like to know more about you."

"Some of us?" he asked, looking at her. The twilight and the energy between them lent a surreal, dreamlike quality to the natural beauty that surrounded them. Did he dare touch her? Or would she ripple and disappear like a mirage? Was her skin as soft and warm as it looked, or was that just the final rays of the sun? And was it the light, or was that lust in her eyes?

"All right. I'd like to know more about you," she said, her heart racing at her boldness. "After all, you will be spending time in my town, with my family."

"Yes, of course," he said, not fooled for a second. His insides twisted into a knot of anticipation, his nerves rattled and snapped with expectation. "Can't be too careful these days. What would you like to know about me?"

She stopped in the middle of the street, turning to him, her breath coming quick and excited. "Everything."

"Everything." He could feel his soul being sucked from him. It was leaving him willingly. Her steady gaze pulled at it gently, without force. She was so beautiful. She was so alive.

If only he would reach out and touch her. He didn't have to kiss her or take her to the ground and ravage her—just touch her anywhere, once. The longing in her was overwhelming and irrational, she knew, but there it was. Just a touch, a simple sign, a . . . what? An indication that he was feeling the same as she? Yes, that's what she wanted. And a single touch would tell her.

He glanced from her eyes to her lips and back again.

Stealing a quick kiss crossed his mind several times in rapid succession before he dismissed it. It wouldn't be quick. And he wouldn't have to steal it, he could see. Her mouth was soft and ripe and waiting. He could feel his heartbeat throbbing in the tips of his fingers, in his knees. If he kissed her, it would be long and slow . . . and it would tear his world apart.

She was a witch, he suspected, leaning toward her. She was casting a spell over him, and he didn't care. He tipped his head closer. He sensed she was the end of the road for him, someone he'd been waiting for, the last woman he'd ever want to kiss. . . . She was incredible. She was . . .

The mother of his brother's child.

He shoved his greedy itching fingers into his pockets and cleared the built-up passion from his throat.

"Well, let's see," he said lightly, turning and walking away from her toward the Hotel, wanting to run. "I had a father and a mother and a brother once, but they've all passed away. I studied government and sociology at Harvard. I have a steady job."

She was acutely aware, and just as disappointed, that the powerful desire she'd sensed moments earlier had somehow cooled, like the desert when the sun wasn't shining on it. It wasn't gone, mind you, it hadn't really changed. It had simply lost its heat.

"I play golf and handball whenever I can. I like to read psycho-thrillers on airplanes. I quit smoking two years ago, and it still makes me a little nuts not to have a cigarette when I want one." Like now. "I've been told that I snore sometimes, but I don't believe it. I think baseball is the longest, most boring sport ever invented, and I'm allergic to penicillin."

He could ignore what he was feeling, but not her.

"And are you married? Or seeing someone special?" she asked, following him up onto the porch in front of the Hotel.

"No," he said, and would have left it at that, except the word just seemed to hang there, waiting. "I have a strange job. I travel a lot. I'm gone all the time. It would be hard on any relationship." He had the urge to kick himself until it was impossible to take another step from her. He wanted the mother of his brother's child. Wanted her so badly he ached. Exerting his will, he turned to her. "And to tell you the truth, I've never met a woman who'd put up with it. Most of them like to have their men home by six-thirty every night. Mine would either have to love to travel or get used to being alone most of the time."

She could see he was battling an inner war. Frustrated need and regret pulled at the fine lines of his face; anger, too, perhaps. But why? Several reasons came to mind. Prior commitment. Disease. Religious beliefs. Social conscience. And scraping the bottom of the barrel, impotence. But it wasn't her, she realized with notable relief. It wasn't that she wasn't his type or not pretty enough. She could see it in his eyes, he did still want her.

"It would be difficult," she said, her curiosity about him doubling, quadrupling. "People tell me that marriage is difficult even when the circumstances are perfect."

"You never married," he said, confounded by this

happenstance. "I mean married again—after the boy's father . . . I would have thought . . . it was a long time ago."

"To tell you the truth, I wasn't married then either," she said, frank and guiltless. "We were going to be married. We felt married. We thought . . . we had more time."

He nodded his understanding. "Still, it was a long time ago."

"It was. I just never . . ." It was hard to explain.

"Found anyone to compare to him?"

"No, that's for sure." She laughed softly. "But that's not all of it. I just never really wanted to, I guess. I had Eric. I was busy. I had all sorts of excuses not to."

"But you might have, if the right man had come along."

She had a feeling that if she let him, he'd dismantle her mind, stone by stone.

"Yeah. Maybe," she acknowledged, taking two steps down off the porch, feeling overexposed all of a sudden. "I might have. But he didn't come along, so . . ."

"So you're still waiting."

"Waiting?" she asked, turning at the bottom of the steps to look up at him. "Waiting for what?"

His smile wasn't unkind, it was unhappy. "For some superman to swoop down and sweep you off your feet."

She laughed out loud then, and it echoed around the basin.

"I'd like to see him try it," she said, amused that he'd think such a thing. "I've already been swept off my feet. And I landed hard on my backside. I'm not easily swept anymore, Mr. Thomas. My roots run deep here, and I'm pretty much set in my ways. This superman would need a forklift or a crane to carry me off." A short pause. "I'll be thirty-one in the fall. I'm not as young or as naive as I once was. I do what I want to do, when I want to do it, the way I want it done. I don't need a man to sweep me off my feet. If I'm waiting for anyone, I'm waiting for a man who will . . . just stand here beside me." She started to walk away then turned back to say, "Good night."

"Good night," he said after several seconds of watching her amble down the dirt road, tall and proud and seriously beautiful in her independence. He leaned against the porch rail and watched till she entered the big metal shop at the far end of town.

Two big blue-and-white Mack trucks, one parked outside and the other halfway inside the large well-lit edifice, made her look small and frail, like a mouse between elephants or an elf between giants. Yet there wasn't a doubt in his mind as to who or what was the bigger, the stronger, and the more powerful.

FOUR

August 11, 1982
Dear Father,

I received your letter several weeks ago. I have read it many times and given it a great deal of thought, not wanting to act in a rash manner or impulsively bite off my own nose to spite my face—a nasty habit of mine that you have often pointed out. The decision I have come to has not been a particularly difficult one. In fact, now that it's finally made, I am relieved.

I am not returning to school. And I am not coming home. Not now. Not anytime soon.

I have been living with a family by the name of Albee. Walter Albee is a good man. He's a truck driver, and he has three sons who help him. He has accepted me into his family, made me feel wanted and capable of contributing something special of my own to it. I will be calling him Dad from now on, as you seem so set on disowning me.

As for your repeated threats to disinherit me, now is as good a time as any. I'm going to marry a sweet, kind, gentle girl who makes me feel richer than any amount of money possibly could. She's pregnant with my baby, and I'm going to stay here and love them both with everything I am or ever hoped to be.

If you are in the mood to grant your condemned son a final request, it would be that you advise my brother of my whereabouts if he should ask about me. And if a last confession is called for, mine is this: I am truly and deeply sorry, Father, that I was unable to please you, in any way, ever.

    Eric

Noah dangled the handwritten letter between two fingers. Then read for the umpteenth time a second, shorter missive found among his father's effects.

March 3, 1983
Dear Mr. Tessler,
I am writing to inform you of the birth of your grandson, Eric Tessler Albee. Born March 1, 1983. In good health.
Sincerely,
Michelin Albee

Holding the notes side by side, he shook his head and tried hard not to be angry—at Eric for being young and proud and stupid, at his father for being old and proud and stupid. At himself for being just plain stupid.

He slipped both letters back into the file folder with the investigator's report, tossing the whole thing onto the dresser as he stood and walked to the window. Nothing to see there. He took several turns around the room, arguing vehemently with two dead men, then walked out the door before he lost his mind completely.

The lights were on downstairs. He probably wasn't in the best of moods to meet his tipsy landlady, but his heart was begging for human companionship, so he couldn't be choosy. He found her in the room where he'd last seen her, and in much the same condition. His hesitation was brief before he snuck over to get a good look at her.

Limp as a fish, she looked as if she'd keeled over, her head coming to rest on the arm of the couch, her feet still on the floor. A woman in her sixties maybe, she had salt-and-pepper hair twisted tightly into a small bun at the nape of her neck. She was as neat and clean as her residence, not a wrinkle marring the front of her long floral dress.

Looking about for burning "see-gars" he noted a full plate of cookies on the coffee table in front of her and a thermos of coffee. For him? he wondered. Had she been expecting him? Her vodka bottle and shot glass were there, too, set carefully on the corner nearest her, and next to that was a clean ashtray with one slim cheroot butt in it.

Suspended animation was the only description he could think of. No doubt about her being a lush, but she also maintained a regular, waking life . . . somehow he just kept missing it.

Easing her feet up onto the couch, he covered her with the afghan as Eric had done that afternoon and then, as if he'd done it a million times before, he screwed the top on the vodka bottle and tiptoed out of the room.

There were no streetlights in Gypsum. A few porch lights were on and a floodlight down at Albee's trucking yard, but the moon was full and bright enough to make it seem like early evening rather than an hour past midnight. There was nowhere to go, nothing to see. No one to engage in lively conversation but the ghosts in his head.

He sat on the steps, bending forward at the waist to rest his head on his arms bridged across his knees.

And that's how she found him, a dark lump on the Hotel steps, alone and somehow sad. Her boots crunched the dirt as she crossed the road, but his mind must have been curled in on itself, much like his body, since he didn't hear her until she was close enough to touch him.

"Too quiet for you?" she asked when he finally looked up. "It's strange what people get used to, isn't it? I go to the city and lie awake all night because of the noise. It never stops."

It wasn't the noise, or the lack of it, that was keeping him up. For weeks now his nights had been plagued with recriminations and regrets. What he needed was peace.

"What's your excuse?" he asked lightly, letting her think whatever she liked. He could hardly look her in the eye, he was so ashamed. Of his family—of himself. How different her life could have been if only he'd taken the time to look for her before now. "You're not still working on that transmission, are you?"

"No," she said, twisting her body sideways without

moving her feet, looking back toward the shop. "I finished that a while ago. Buck is gone already. He has a load of lettuce to pick up by noon tomorrow. Actually, I . . ." She paused to look up at the Hotel. "I was just on my way to bed. I thought maybe I'd turn out the lights for Greta."

Turning on the step, he could see the Hotel was lit up like a paper lantern behind him.

"Oh. I hadn't . . ." He hadn't realized they were on, or he'd have turned them off earlier. "I'll do it when I go in."

"She's asleep, I take it?"

He nodded, turning back to her. "On the couch. Like a baby," he said, his voice still brittle with his frustrations.

Mich glanced at the Hotel door, thinking of the woman who lived behind it, then back to the man on the steps, who knew nothing about her.

"You shouldn't judge her too harshly," she said softly. "People have reasons for doing what they do, for the way they live their lives."

"I wasn't. I . . .." he began, realizing what he must sound like. She and the boy were the innocents in this mess, and as much as he wanted to share the truth with her, she didn't deserve the rancor that went with it. "I'm sorry. I'm not in a very good mood."

"Then I'm sorry. Is there anything I can do? Do you feel like talking?"

Yes. He needed to talk about it. He wanted to tell her everything.

"No. But thanks. It's . . . nothing really. Business."

"Oh." They were both surprised by how disappointed she sounded. She smiled. "Well, how about I give you some good news? Think that'll help?"

"Couldn't hurt." How could anyone not respond to a face like that? he wondered once again, smiling back at her. It would be so easy to get lost in those dark eyes, to bury himself in the curvaceous comforts of her body. What he wouldn't give to get his arms around her. . . .

"Your belt will be here in the morning."

"What?"

"The belt? For your car? It'll be here in the morning." She forced herself to smile. "Eric seems to have taken a real liking to you. He called Frank back—our distributor?—and told him to go ahead and Express Mail the belt we need. It should be here before noon."

"Oh, well . . . That was nice of him." Was wringing a nephew's neck allowed in Uncledom? "Very nice."

She laughed halfheartedly. "He seemed pretty pleased with himself. Surprised me," she added as an afterthought.

"Why?"

She shrugged and looked up at the brightly lit windows of the Hotel. "I don't know, I thought he was looking forward to spending some time with you. Talking with you. He said . . . well, I guess he thought getting you back on the road would make you happier than hanging around here."

He nodded.

"He does the strangest things sometimes," she went on absently, wondering if she dared tinker with the inlet valves in his carburetor or change the timing on his alternator.

Both were so intent, thinking about the same thing, that long moments passed in silence. Mich had rubbed a small rut in the road with the toe of her boot.

"Well," she said abruptly, feeling foolish. "I guess I should go. I have a car to work on in the morning."

He looked up at her. The passion and desire in his eyes was so unexpected and so penetrating, she stopped breathing. Her heart quit beating. She took an instinctive step backward.

"Thank you," he said, balling his hands into fists between his knees. He had to stay seated. If he stood up, he'd snatch her into his arms and never let go. "For the good news. For dinner tonight. For everything."

"No problem." She flapped her arms against her thighs as she took several more steps away from him, her chest aching as her heart started up again. "It's all part of Albee Towing. . . . Serving the greater part of eastern Nevada. Open twenty-four hours a day . . ."

"Fast friendly service guaranteed."

She stopped. "No. Not always. We can't guarantee fast. And we never guarantee friendly." One was a matter of luck and the other was earned. "But we'll give you your money back if you're not satisfied with the work."

He accepted the offer with a nod and an ironic smile.

"Good night, Michelin."

"Good night."

Releasing the latch and lifting the hood of the Escort sounded like the squeaky attic door in a low-budget mystery movie—plenty loud enough to wake the dead, or the sleeping town of Gypsum.

Bending over the engine, he had only the moonlight to help him, and no mystical moonbeam was shining on anything particular so as to give him a clue as to what to tamper with. Beating it with a hammer seemed a little too obvious, yet anything less could be too easy for Michelin to fix. Draining the battery? No, she'd simply jump-start it. What he needed was a *real* mechanical problem.

"Why did you come here?"

Noah spun around on his heel and staggered back against the car, adrenaline flowing, muscles snapping, ready to ward off an attack.

"If she knew who you were, she'd shoot you."

Eric and Lug stepped from the shadow beside the garage, and relief washed over Noah like a pail of cold water. His hand automatically reached up to soothe his quaking heart, then he leaned back on the radiator, not bothering to hide his displeasure at being ambushed.

"Don't ever do that again," he said. "Another person might not be as glad to see you as I am."

"You don't sound glad to see me," Eric said, secretly admiring his uncle's recuperative powers.

"Give me a second, I'm working on it." He tried to make out the boy's expression in the moonlight. "Mentioning the Diplomatic Corps, that's what tipped you off, right?"

"That and all the questions." A brief pause. "And the way you kept looking at me."

He nodded, accepting the fact that duplicity wasn't his forte. "So, why don't you blow the whistle on me?"

"I don't want my mom hurt again. It'll be better if you just leave before she figures it out." Again he hesitated. "There are pictures, you know. In a box in her closet. You look like him."

"So do you."

They were connected whether Eric wanted them to be or not. And if he was any sort of judge, Noah sensed that he didn't really mind too much, that the boy was drawn to him—but his mother's feelings stood between them.

"Why *did* you come here?" he asked finally, stepping closer.

"To meet you and your mother. Get to know you."

"What for?"

"You're my nephew. I'm your uncle. And as of two months ago, you and I are what's left of the Tessler family. You're all the family I have left."

Eric turned his head and looked down the dark empty street. "My grandfather's dead?"

"Yes."

It was hard to tell what, if anything, this meant to the boy as he nodded his head and looked everywhere but at Noah.

"Eric," he said, and waited for the boy to look at him. It was confession time. "I didn't know about you. I didn't know you existed until I went through my father's papers. I found a letter from my brother and one from your mother." The boy simply stared at him. He waved a hand helplessly. "There is no excuse. . . . I *have* a million of them, of course, but . . . but there's no excuse good enough for what's happened. I . . .

never dreamed, so I never asked. And he never told me."

"How did he die?" was all Eric said.

"Old age mostly, his heart gave out." It seemed humorous, almost, that the lump of stone that did the duty of a heart in his father's chest should be his undoing.

"So now you've come to take me away," the boy said, making an assumption.

"Take you away?"

"From my mom. You came here to make sure she was a bad mother and to get lawyers to take me away from her," he said, his voice venomous in the dark. "Well, you can just go to hell, mister, because I'm not going. And if you try to kidnap me, I'll run away. First chance I get."

"What the hell are you talking about?"

"That's why you came here, isn't it? That's why you lied about who you were and . . . and I bet there was never anything wrong with your stupid old car."

"Eric, no," he said, stunned by the boy's reaction. He'd been prepared for the anger but not for the fear. "I haven't come here to take you away. I didn't come to hurt you or your mother. That's the last thing I want to do."

"Then why'd you lie? Why'd you sneak in here pretending to be somebody else?"

Noah let loose a sigh of frustration. He didn't know why anymore.

"I thought if I wrote ahead and told you I was coming, you'd act different. Treat me different, like a guest. You'd be on your best behavior. I guess I thought that if you didn't know who I was at first, you'd act more naturally, that we could become friends and . . . then I'd tell you."

"Or catch us off guard. Catch my mom doing something that would make her look like a bad mother . . ."

"No," he said firmly. "No. That was never my intention. I wouldn't dream of taking you from her." He faltered. "What the hell would I do with you?"

This cut through Eric's fear and had him thinking. "What would my grandfather have done with me if he'd gotten me?"

"Your grandfather tried to take you away from your mother?"

He saw the boy's head nod. "When I was a baby. He said bad things about my mom. And my granddad. They had to go to court. He said because my mom never married my dad that she was bad, and she didn't have a lot of money and all my uncles except Otis drank too much and got into fights. But none of that was true. My mom got legal custody of me so my grandfather couldn't come and take me away from her."

Noah felt a heaviness in his chest and had an uncommon urge to cry. In fact, he had to blink back tears, and his throat was so tight, he couldn't speak, even if he'd known what to say.

Eric seemed to sense his suffering and, after several minutes, continued. "She's always been afraid he would take me away," he said, calmer, taking several more steps toward Noah and the car. "That's why I can't talk to strangers unless someone's around. That's why she home-taught me and why she wants to send me away to that prison school in the fall."

"Prison school?"

"You know. One of those fancy private prep schools where everyone wears a uniform and there are guards at the front gate." He looked down at the exposed engine. "She took me to see it last spring, but I'm not goin'. I'm not going to Harvard or Yale or any of those fancy colleges either. No offense, but I'd rather go to Nevada State or maybe Arizona. I don't care what she says. What were you trying to do here?" he asked, frowning over the motor.

"Stall for more time," he said, slowly digesting all he'd heard. "Some *busybody* ordered my fan belt Express Mail, so I needed to figure out some other way to stay here."

"Well, now you can just tell her who you are and stay as long as you want."

"You think it'll be that easy?" he asked. "What do you think she'll do when I tell her?"

Eric considered this for a moment. "Shoot you." Noah frowned and shifted his stance uncomfortably. "She won't believe you. That you just came to meet us. She'll think you're up to something."

This wasn't what he'd wanted. He never meant to scare Eric and sure didn't want to frighten Michelin.

"Maybe I should leave in the morning," he said, discouraged. He could handle the business end of this trip by mail and leave them both in peace. "I don't want to cause any trouble."

"No. Stay." Eric was firm about this. "With my grandfather gone and you not wanting to take me away, I might not have to go to that fancy school after all. I could go to a regular high school. We just need to pick the right time to tell her. You know, so she doesn't go off."

"Go off?"

Eric looked at him. "She has a temper," he confided. "Granddad says she got it from her mom. He says that if his first wife had a temper like that, he'd have three sons in prison by now."

"So your uncles are pretty mellow." Good news at last!

"No. They have tempers, too, just not like Mom's."

"Swell." He sighed, resigned to being shot or beaten to a pulp. "So, what should I do now?"

In the end, it was Eric who stuffed several old grease cloths high up the tailpipe of the Escort with a broom handle, packing them tight. "This'll drive her crazy for at least two or three days. The exhaust will back up and choke the engine. She won't know if it's the electrical system or the distributor or the carbeurator or the fuel system or—"

"I get the picture," Noah said, thinking there was more of his brother in Eric than he'd first imagined. Creative mischief had been his trademark. Still, he couldn't help admiring the boy's mechanical savvy. "Did you learn this from working with your mother?"

"Nah. This is just basic combustion stuff. No oxygen, no fire. First-grade stuff."

He turned a blinding grin to Noah in the moonlight. It had "You Dummy" written all over it, and he started to giggle.

FIVE

"I just don't understand it," she kept saying after re-placing the belt. "It doesn't make sense. What do you think, Dad? He's got spark. And I checked the fuel line."

Walt took off his cap with two fingers and ran the rest of them over his hair, scowling at the motor in question. Noah stood between them with his hands on his hips, shaking his head and muttering false encouragement.

"Don't know, Mich," Walt said in a voice that would no doubt be an avalanche hazard at a higher altitude. "Looks to me like you're gonna have to break it apart, take a good look-see at everything. Could take some time."

Father and daughter looked at each other, then at Noah, who felt suddenly pushed into the spotlight.

"Oh. Well. You two are the pros here. If you have to take it apart, you have to take it apart."

"It's going to take time," Mich reiterated, pretty

sure she could repair the valves she'd jammed in his carburetor in a day if he gave the slightest indication that he was impatient to be on his way.

"No problem," he said cheerfully. "Eric's promised me another basketball game after his lessons. It might take the better part of a week to finally beat him—and I'm not leaving till I do, so take your time."

"Are you sure?" she asked, swallowing the giddy laughter in her throat, afraid to pat herself on the back too soon. "If Dad and I both work on it—"

"No no. Really. I'm fine here. I'm in no hurry. You aren't trying to get rid of me, are you?"

Walt laughed and laid one of his huge paws on Noah's shoulder. "You two make up your minds on this, I got work of my own waitin'. For my part, I wouldn't mind havin' you around awhile."

"Well, thank you," Noah said, vastly pleased, watching him walk away and fully understanding his brother's fondness for the big, gentle man. He shifted his gaze to meet Michelin's. "What about you? Will you mind having me around for a while?"

"No, of course not," she said, hard put not to wiggle head to toe like a happy puppy. "I'm looking forward to knowing you better."

Instinctively his eyes narrowed and his look intensified, searched, and questioned. A double entendre? Could he take that to mean anything he wanted it to? When she didn't look away, a slow provocative smile came to his lips.

"Me too."

"Pretend you don't see her."

Instantly red-faced, Noah looked back at Eric just as the basketball bounced off his chest. It wasn't the first time he'd been distracted from the game. But how could he possibly pretend not to see her? he wondered, glancing back at Michelin's long legs and very fine tush as she bent over the Escort's engine.

It was hotter than a camel's saddle, but waiting till late afternoon afforded them the relief of a square block of shade behind the gas station.

Eric came to stand beside him, scooping up the ball on his way. "If you don't look at her, you can pretend you don't hear her."

As they stood facing Michelin it occurred to Noah that perhaps they were speaking of someone else.

"She's behind us now?"

"Almost. She's coming down the street on her bike."

Now the question was, how could he possibly not look at *anyone* he was told not to look at?

Unfortunately, by the time he'd batted the ball from Eric's hands, dribbled twice, and dared a quick curious glance in her direction, the girl had come to a stop not thirty feet away to watch them—and he made direct eye contact with her.

"Hi," she said with a wide gap-toothed grin. "Can I play?"

Eric groaned and mumbled something, casting a killing glare in Noah's direction. God help him, couldn't he do anything right? This uncle business was tricky, and he wanted to be good at it.

"Hi, there," he said, smiling kindly at who could

only be Corie Wilks—an adolescent female, despite Eric's doubts, with a short golden crop of curls, big bright sky-blue eyes, and what appeared to be some mildly interesting developments under the baggy cotton T-shirt she wore. "We were just—"

"We're playing one-on-one," Eric stated rudely, tossing the ball back to Noah to take it out.

"But we were just saying that if someone else came along," Michelin said, walking over with a pointed look at her son, "we could play doubles. Isn't that right, Eric?"

After all, one could only lean over an engine simulating repairs, switching tools occasionally for effect, craning her neck to watch a fantastic male body in action for so long before she felt compelled to get closer to it.

His laughter was a lure that curved her lips and teased her spirits. It didn't occurr to her to question Eric's sudden about-face toward their guest. He was as fickle as a weather vane these days, and she simply assumed he was as charmed as she was by Noah.

She was delighted to see Corie, glad, in fact, she'd thought to call her.

Eric met his mother's gaze. "Guys against girls?" he asked, stacking the deck.

"Absolutely."

She winked at Corie. Eric grinned confidently at his uncle as he scratched the top of Lug's head. A coin was tossed for first out.

Noah was sweating like a pig in a matter of minutes. "You don't play fair," he told Mich, breathless as he pushed himself up out of the dirt for the third time. She had a body block like a stone wall.

"Of course I do," she said, stepping up to the hoop for a perfect bank shot. "Albees are nothing if not fair." She watched the ball swish, then turned her head and grinned at him. "I just don't play like a girl."

No, she played like Dennis Rodman. Yacking, distracting, and with no apologies.

"And that's not fair," he said, hands on his hips as he gasped for air. "I can't play that rough with you."

She laughed out loud, and as he was no threat at present, she helped Corie double-block Eric's next shot, saying, "Why not? Are you physically unable to or"—a grunt of exertion—"are you being a gentleman?"

It was both, actually.

"Don't be a gentleman, man," Eric said ruthlessly. "I'm playing by myself here. Run her down. She's killing us."

She laughed again. The sound tickled Noah's soul.

"Leave him alone, Eric," she said. "I don't mind if he wants to be a gentleman." She dribbled the ball past him deliberately, dodged Eric as if she'd been doing it for years, and sank the ball again. "Although, to be fair, if he's going to play that way, I should probably tie one hand behind my back."

Was she goading him? Yes she was, he could see, as something wild inside him rose to the occasion. He found it much less strenuous simply to play the game than to play the game constantly trying not to make body contact. As a matter of fact, the body contact made the game downright delightful.

Delightful to the point of distraction, he noticed as

she kept her back to him, using her butt to push him away. It didn't immediately occurr to him that she was completely aware of what she doing or that he was re-acting exactly as she wanted him to, but when it did, he stood at center court and gaped at her.

"You call that fair?" he asked, more than half-amused.

She laughed. "I call that using all my best assets. Playing to my potential. You don't want me to *let* you win, do you? How fair would that be?"

She was standing in front of him, arms extended, waving side to side to cover as much of his shooting space as possible when she heard Eric call to her. The tone of his voice halted her.

Putting her hands on Noah's waist, she bent under his raised arms to peer around him at the big rig and trailer parked in the middle of the street at the far end of town.

With two burning handprints still sizzling against his ribs, Noah followed her as she walked away to stand beside Eric.

"The Carlsons," Corie said, sounding ominous as she went to stand next to Eric too. "They have a lot of nerve." The three of them stood staring at the copper-colored Freightliner. Noah squinted against the sun to see it more clearly; to ascertain its importance.

"That's not nerve," Eric said, disgusted. "That's stupid. What do they think they're doing?"

"They're trying to intimidate me," Mich said quietly, almost absently. "Wear me down."

"Why?" Noah asked. But his question was drowned

out as the truck's engine revved, mocking their lack of response to its presence in the street.

"Man," Eric said like a curse word. "Why don't you just give her a pull and get it over with? Break her stupid arm."

She glanced at her son, then lowered her eyes to the ground before looking back at the truck. "I'll wait for the tournament."

"What tournament?" Noah asked, once again losing out to the truck's engine.

"You can take her easy, Mich," Corie said, then with the tiniest hint of doubt in her voice, she asked, "Can't you?"

"Of course she can," Eric said, turning his anger on the girl because she was conveniently close . . . and asking dumb questions to boot. "But there's no sense in beating her twice when once is all Mom needs to win the regionals. She just wants Mom to fight her early so she won't have to lose in front of all those people. Mom'll take her at the tournament, and that'll shut her up once and for all."

"Shut who up?" Noah asked, shouting to be heard over the engine. The three of them turned to look at him. "What's all this about?"

"The Southwestern Regional Arm-Wrestling Tournament," Corie said.

"Mom's going to enter this year," Eric added.

"That's why the Carlsons are so mad," Corie tacked on. "Lola Carlson has been women's regional champion three years in a row, but she never wins at the nationals."

"Yeah, and Mom's beat her all three years down at

the Saloon. For fun. No bets or anything." He turned back to the truck. "Lola's scared spitless."

Noah had almost all the information he'd asked for, but realized none of it had come from Michelin.

"You're an arm wrestler?" he asked, trying very hard to keep the amused astonishment out his voice as he thought of huge hairy women on steroids and compared them with her.

"Not professionally, until now," she said, turning her back on the Carlsons altogether and walking back to the hoop. She was looking a little self-conscious for the first time since Noah had met her, and he found it very endearing. "My brother Roy has been to the world tournament four times, but I . . . mostly I wrestle for fun, down at the Saloon sometimes."

She hesitated. The look on his face was hard to decipher. He was either terribly taken aback or terribly intrigued. And she was feeling terribly . . . butch. "I'm strong and I wrestle men most the time," she told him honestly, refusing to feel shame for anything she was good at. "But I don't know about competing in the women's pro division. Most of them are bodybuilders. They're smart and they have really good techniques. I watched them last year. Compared to them, my amateur standing sticks out all over."

He was still finding it hard to take this new revelation seriously. Arm wrestling? A child's game, right?

The Carlsons, having used up what time they thought they could spare on their manifest, put the truck into gear and started toward them slowly. A man was driving, and the woman riding shotgun displayed a rather crude hand gesture from the side window as they passed by.

"Eric," Mich said, in a cautioning voice when his hand shot into the air, turning a similar gesture into a fake-friendly wave.

They used the truck yard to turn around, then sped out of town, stirring a cloud of dust that took several minutes to settle again.

"When they come back, I'm going to throw rotten tomatoes at 'em," Eric said, mindlessly bouncing the ball.

"Do you know for sure that they're coming back?" Noah asked, fascinated, dying to see what would happen next.

She nodded. "If their load is for Reno, they'll be back sometime tonight. If they're heading all the way to California, it'll be tomorrow or the next day. But they'll be back."

"And here you thought I was going to be bored," he said, grinning mischievously when she looked at him. The puzzled relief in her expression pulled at him. "When is this tournament?"

"A week from Friday. In Flagstaff."

"Maybe you could hang around and go with her," Eric suggested with a significant look at his uncle.

"Eric!" she said, giving a startled half laugh. "He's passing through. He's got business to take care of and . . . and backtracking to Flagstaff would throw him even further off schedule."

It was Thursday. That gave him plenty of time to explain things to her and, if she wasn't too angry with him, maybe wheedle a personal invitation to the tournament.

"Don't worry," she said, seeing his concern. "I'll have your car fixed and you back on the road long before next Friday."

"I wasn't worried," he said. "I was trying to remember if I'd ever been to Arizona? And you know what? I don't think I have."

"So why have you picked now to turn professional arm wrestler?" he asked her, shooting a little lighter fluid on the charcoal briquets lying on the bottom of the barbecue he'd offered to light.

Eric had also invited him to dinner, explaining that aside from Max's chicken specials, his mother's food was the best in town. She'd laughed, accepted this small claim to fame, and encouraged him to come.

She handed him a box of stick matches. "I need the money. The prize is only five thousand at the regionals, but it's twenty-five thousand at the nationals, and fifty thousand at the world tournament."

"That's a lot of money," he said, striking a match. It fizzled out immediately.

"The men compete for a hundred thousand."

"That's a lot of money too."

"And private prep schools cost a lot of money," she said, watching him hunker over the coals, strike a match, and lay it on a briquet. She really liked watching his hands. . . .

They both watched the match burn itself out.

Mich picked up the lighter fluid and squeezed a lot

into the barbecue, then stepped back and closed her eyes as Noah tossed a lick of fire in after it.

The *poof* and smoke and raging flames were gratifying to them both. They smiled together. Their gazes met and held as the fire raged.

Her heart raced as he studied her face, desire softening the intensity of his expression. A single glance at her mouth had her lips tingling with anticipation. Slowly, she raised her hand to his rough, barely stubbled cheek and held her breath as he leaned his face into it, his eyelids drooping as if it were causing him extreme pleasure or pain.

He pulled away abruptly, glanced at the box of matches in his hands as if he wasn't sure what they were, then held them out to her.

An awkward moment passed between them in which one knew she should demand an explanation and the other was aware he should say something, but simply couldn't.

"Eric," he said finally, tossing the name out like a crucifix before a vampire. "He and I talked a little about his education this morning," he said, being careful not to touch her as he pushed the box into her hands, sure that if he did, he'd fall apart like a mountain of ash. "I had no idea home teaching could be so progressive and thorough," he said, striving for a casual air. "Or that so much of it could be done by computer. He said there was an alternative teaching group you belong to, and you get together once a month for outings and social events. He even showed me how he talks to his pals on a local hyperterminal."

He followed Mich into the house. He'd taken a

great deal of comfort from the conversation he'd had with Eric, but it wasn't until she turned to face him across the kitchen counter that he realized *their* conversation was having the exact opposite effect on her.

"Really," he said, reacting to the expression on her face. "I'm impressed. He showed me the results of his national equivalency tests. He's above his age and grade level in everything." He hesitated. "You must be very proud of him."

She stared at him so long without sound or expression that he was beginning to think he'd overstepped himself. Then, as if she's been holding her breath, she burst out laughing and shook her head.

"Do you know that kid has sent my father and all three of my brothers in here, one at a time, to tell me how well he did on his last equivalency tests? And now you?"

"Well, he doesn't want to go away to school. Especially to one of those prison schools," he said, spurting out the words Eric had used, recalling the eight years he spent at Canyon River Military Academy. His brother had arrived in the fall of Noah's senior year, and leaving him there in the spring, as a young, shy fifth grader, had been one of the hardest things he'd ever done. "I know it's none of my business but—"

"You're right," she said, not unkindly, despite the instant headache she got every time the subject came up. "It isn't any of your business. But since Eric has roped you in on this, I'll explain it to him—through you —one more time." She opened the refrigerator and took out salad fixings, setting them on the counter one after another as she spoke. "I don't want to send him

away to school. I love him. I like having him around."
She stopped mid-motion to look at him directly. "You
tell him that. Tell him I love him more than anything
else on earth. He doesn't seem to believe me."

Noah couldn't help smiling a little at that. If Eric
knew anything, it was that he was loved. *Not* knowing if
you were loved made communicating your resentment
impossible, made leaving all that much easier. Noah
knew this from experience.

"Then remind him that I have an obligation, a duty,
a responsibility to make sure that he gets the best possible education that money can buy," she said, trying to
remain calm. "That includes that snooty prep school
and one of those fancy Ivy League universities back
east." She slammed a stalk of celery down on the
counter. "And you tell him it's as much his responsibility as it is mine. . . . No, no, don't tell him that. It's
not his responsibility, it's mine. Just mine."

By now Noah's brows were joined in the middle,
and he was completely confused. He stepped around the
counter and boldly removed the knife she was waving
around and set it beside the vegetables.

"You think I'm crazy, don't you?" she asked. He
could feel her trembling as he held her hands between
his own. "I'm not. I just wish someone would believe
that this is as hard on me as it is on him. I'm not the bad
guy here. I have to do what I think is best for him,
whether it's what I want or not."

"But are you sure that sending him away is the best
thing for him? Gypsum is a weird little place but—"

"You don't understand." She removed her hands
from his and turned back to the salad. She could hardly

think straight with him standing so close. "Eric's father wasn't just some drifter, some bum on a motorcycle passing through town. He came from a wealthy Chicago family." She watched her hand turning the handle of the knife around and around. "There were . . . problems in the family. Not much love . . . He was only nineteen and he'd run away from school and he wouldn't go home." She looked up and once again was struck by how much of a comfort it was to talk to the man across from her, with his perceptive expression, the compassion in his eyes. "We were very much in love, but even then I knew that he'd never be happy, not truly and completely happy, if he couldn't resolve things with his father and brother."

"His brother?" The words were out before he could stop them. It had been one of his few comforts, all these years, that he and Eric had parted on good terms. They'd had things to resolve?

"They ignored Eric. That was his name too. Eric," she said, calm enough finally to control her hands. She started washing leaves of lettuce off in the sink—didn't see the pained expression on Noah's face. "The only way he could get their attention was to do something terrible. Get kicked out of school. Run away. Steal something. The brother would show up to bail him out of whatever trouble he was in, but after a while even he stopped coming. He was some sort of foreign diplomat, overseas all the time. He couldn't be bothered with Eric anymore, I guess." She sighed and started in on the radishes. "Anyway, by the time he showed up here, the situation between him and his family was pretty awful. Dad tried to talk to him about it, but he was young and stubborn and hurt . . . he didn't want anything to do with them anymore."

Noah had taken a seat at the kitchen table, lost in thoughts of his own.

"What does any of that have to do with sending your son away to school?" he asked. Having failed his brother, the least he could do was to stand by his brother's son.

"Eric could have been anything he wanted to be," she said finally, walking across the small kitchen to sit in a chair across from him. "He was smart, and he'd been well educated. His family was powerful." She studied the towel in her hands for several seconds before going on. "When he died we called his father to let him know. We never did talk to him directly, but that very night there were all sorts of people here, secretaries and assistants and lawyers. They packed up Eric's body and took him away to bury him in Chicago. The lawyer, Mr. Tessler's lawyer, was a horrible man. He kept saying that if we hadn't encouraged Eric in his defiance of his father, they would have reconciled and he wouldn't have been here and he wouldn't have died. . . . Not in so many words, but he implied it. They all did. They were rude and mean and treated us like dirt. And then . . ."

She set the towel aside and clasped her hands together in front of her as if to get a firm hold on herself. "Well, when Eric was born I wasn't sure what to do, but I felt like Mr. Tessler ought to know about him, so I wrote and told him he had a grandson. That was a huge mistake." She tipped her head to one side and spoke thoughtfully. "Dad tried to tell me that Mr. Tessler felt guilty for the way he'd treated his son and wanted to make it up to his grandson, but . . ." She shook her head in disbelief. "He tried to take Eric away from me. Legally. I was just seventeen and unmarried, not finished with high school. If it hadn't been for Dad and Greta, Max and the others, I would have lost Eric." She reached for the towel again, twisted the threads on the end to occupy her restless hands. "They stood up for me. Lent me money for the lawyers. Gypsum is a weird little town, like you said, but the people here are the best you'll find anywhere. I owe them my life."

After a few minutes she went on.

"The thing is," she said, frowning. "Even though I won, there were things said at the trial that stuck with me all these years."

"Like what?" he asked, praying it wasn't that she was an immoral person, a bad mother, or any of the other garbage he was sure his father's lawyers had made her out to be. It wasn't hard for him to envision the young girl she'd been, facing an army of highly trained and extremely vicious lawyers with her son in her arms.

"Well, at one point, the lawyer was saying that Eric was so young and immature that if he hadn't died, he would have come to his senses and reconciled with his father and raised his son with all the advantages the Tessler family had to offer. And, well, I know it sounds a little crazy, but I think he might have. Given more time, he might have made up with his father. I think, deep down, he wanted to. He might have wanted Eric to go to prep schools the way he did. And to Harvard like his older brother had. He might have wanted those things for Eric, when he was older, when he was more mature . . . he might have."

"So you think you owe it to Eric's father to send him away to school." His heart was twisted so tight inside his chest, it was numb. Even the knowledge that he could relieve her misery was no comfort to him, so vivid was the pain from the past. "You think there's some sort of tradition you should maintain in his memory."

She shrugged. "Sort of." A big sigh. "I hate them so much."

"Who?" he asked, knowing full well who.

"The Tesslers. What sort of people are they?" she asked, as if he might know someone like them. "What sort of people would take a baby away from his mother? What sort of family ignores each other like that? Even that brother I told you about, he never once wrote or called about his nephew. I always thought that he might. Eric loved him. He said he could be counted on, that he'd gone off to live his own life but that he'd be back someday. I never did understand their relationship, but I never heard a word from him. It was as easy for him to walk away from his nephew as it was to walk away from his brother."

"You don't know that," he said in his own defense. "I mean . . . something could have happened, something that prevented him from—"

"Don't get me wrong," she broke in. "I'm glad he never showed up. If he's anything like his father, I'd have to kill him on sight. I would." She got up and went back to making the salad for their dinner. "Well, I would have when Eric was younger. Now he's old enough to understand things. He knows I love him and that he belongs with me, that's why I think it's safe to send him away to school now. He won't leave with anyone he doesn't know without putting up a good fight."

"So all these years you've been afraid someone would abduct Eric," he said. The boy had said as much the night before, but he sensed there was more. "That's why you never tried to leave Gypsum. And why you home taught him instead of busing him to Warm Springs or Ely."

"I know it sounds paranoid, but you read about it all the time. Parents stealing their own children from each other, grandparents stealing them, disappearing with them. And the Tesslers have a lot of money. Mr. Tessler has a lot of power, in Chicago anyway. I couldn't risk it."

He should have told her then and there that William F. Tessler had no power. Not in Chicago, not anywhere anymore. Real or imagined he was no longer a threat to her.

But he didn't. Couldn't.

He *would*. Of course he *would*—but he wanted to explain who he was first, break it to her gently. And, come to think of it, he wanted her to be so in love with him that it wouldn't matter to her who he was. . . . That's what he wanted. And that's what he hoped he had a one-in-a-million chance of achieving.

Oh, he knew honesty was the best policy and that there would be a price to pay for his deception. He knew he'd fallen in love with the woman who had once given her heart to his brother, and that he was already deeply in arrears to both of them. He even knew that his debts might be too far beyond his means ever to repay.

If nothing else, he wasn't lying to himself anymore.

SIX

The desert was awesome in its desolation. Hauntingly beautiful as the setting sun once again bathed the grim wilderness in warm hues of pink and lavender. It was the sixth such sunset Noah had observed from Gypsum, each different, each magnificent, each a reminder of another day gone by in which he'd lied, evaded, procrastinated, and in general . . . blown it.

Not that he didn't have good excuses for blowing his chances to tell the truth. The afternoon the Carlsons returned to town was a little too tense a time to broach the subject.

"Say what you want, Lola," Mich said calmly, sitting at a table in the middle of the Saloon, her long legs crossed, her foot swinging lazily. It was a deceptive pose, he knew, as she'd been tense and dreading the confrontation when they walked down the street together to meet the husband-and-wife team just moments before. "Call me any name you can think of, I'm not going to wrestle you till Friday."

"Well, don't be thinking that just because I let you beat me a couple times in the past that I won't give you my full arm at the tournament. I've been working out."

"Oh, I expect to get your whole arm. I expect you'll break mine, but you're still going to have to wait till Friday."

The conversation continued, and Noah backed up to the bar to sit beside Walt, who sat passively watching the incident in the mirror behind the bar.

"They're all so serious about this arm wrestling," Noah commented. "They're like a bunch of prizefighters."

Walt turned his head to give him a good look over, then looked back at the mirror. "There are those who think arm wrestling ought to be included as an Olympic sport. They think it's a truer competition between two contestants. One-on-one, no fancy equipment, just muscle and wit. Truth be told, I'd rather watch a good pull than a Ping-Pong game."

Noah glanced back at the women and saw a whole new scenario. Mich with her gracefully strong body, Lola Carlson with the corded muscles in her arms and shoulders, the challenge and determination in their expressions.

"The women turn out to be the most interesting to watch," Walt added. "The girl says it's because they have more to lose."

The older man squinted his wrinkled eyelids in thought. "It's like they got more respect for each other, for the game, for themselves. They're good sports. Not but a few like this one here," he said, using his head to nod in Lola Carlson's direction. "Puts the whole thing in a bad light, when they act like that."

"Beating me once or twice don't make you nothing," Lola was saying. "I didn't give you my full arm. I felt sorry for ya in this dinky town, no real competition 'cept Roy. And he babies you too."

"Roy always beats me. He's twice my size," Mich said with a shrug, though you could tell from her expression that her exasperation level was climbing.

Lola laughed. "Jake ain't twice your size. And he could take you easy."

Mich's eyes shifted to the woman's husband. Jake was not a big man, to be sure, and not one of the regular wrestlers, his hobbies leaning more toward womanizing, toll dodging, and unlogged runs. But he gave her a thought.

"Do you practice with Jake?" she asked Lola.

" 'Course. *We* truck for a livin'. And we got more than one kid. Can't spend all my time looking for good pulls."

"Do you beat him every time?"

Lola looked at her husband, then back to Mich. "Not every time. No. He's a man, he's stronger."

"Then would you say he's a fair pull? Someone I might win if I was at least as good as you?"

Once again, Lola's gaze slid toward Jake, and she shifted her weight nervously as she began to understand what Mich was getting at.

"Yeah, I'd say he was a fair pull," she said, knowing he beat her nine out of ten times. All she usually hoped for in playing him was a good workout. "He's a real good pull."

Jake sent a close-lipped smile in his wife's direction but said nothing.

"Let's make a deal, then," Mich said, getting to her feet. "If I beat Jake, you drop out of the regionals."

"And when you lose?"

"Then at least you'll know you have a good chance at beating me on Friday."

Husband and wife exchanged glances and a slight nod, and no further words seemed necessary. Jake pushed himself away from the bar and all three started walking toward the back to a structure designed specifically for arm wrestling—an adjustable table that came up to their midsections with an elbow cup and grip for the opposite hand.

It was about this time that Eric, having finished his lessons and seeing the big Freightliner parked in front of the Saloon, came bursting in on the scene. Noting which two people were stretching their muscles, swinging their arms, and flexing their fingers, he came to an immediate conclusion.

"Mom, no," he said, anger contorting his young face.

"Hush now, boy," Walt said. "The girl knows what she's doing."

"She does?" Noah asked, not liking the looks of Jake.

"You come on over here," Walt said to Eric. And when he'd joined them at the bar, he added in his low-loud tones. "Take a good look, boy. That character look any bigger or stronger than our Otis?"

A slow sly smile spread across Eric's face as he studied the man's shape and size. He relaxed visibly. A glance at his uncle had him chuckling.

"It's okay," he said. "There's a good chance she can beat him, and no chance he can hurt her arm."

"He's bigger than she is."

"Yeah, but it doesn't matter. He's top-heavy like Otis, so he probably doesn't have a solid center of gravity. Mom does. When the time is right, she can reset her grip, throw him off balance, and take him over the top. Weight distribution," he said, and grinned. "A man the same size with better weight distribution could break her arm or throw her shoulder out of joint. There's a lot more to it than just size and strength."

"So I'm beginning to understand," Noah said, wondering about his own weight distribution, where his center of gravity was, what he'd do if Michelin ever challenged him.

The Carlsons, too, learned about weight distribution that day, stomping out of the Saloon some three minutes later, muttering angrily at each other and knocking over a chair as they went.

The main event took all of maybe thirty seconds—gripping and taking a stance not included. Lola called the "go." Muscles flexed, grimaces contorted their faces, and suddenly the back of Jake's arm was on the table, Michelin's on top.

Then, of course, Mich was too pumped up, too giddy, too very cute and peacocky in her triumph to be told the man she was strutting around for was a liar and a cheat.

"You just don't want to mess with an Albee on a Saturday afternoon," she crowed, her eyes dancing with delight. "Sodas and french fries all round, Chuckie. On me. And none of that watered-down ketchup you serve to the tourists. We want the real stuff."

After dinner that night, they sat outside in lawn chairs enjoying the perfection between the heat of the day and the chill of the night. A gigantic moon smiled down on them as they listened to Walt tell stories about Mich and young Eric. It was simply too nice, too pleasant a time to tell her. . . .

"Didn't know what to do with her when she first arrived, the first Albee female born in sixty-five years," Walt said proudly, adding, "I named her after my favorite steel-belted radial tire."

Noah wanted to laugh aloud, not because she'd been named after a tire but because he hadn't realized it before, thinking it an unusual, exotic, Gallic name instead.

"I admit I was still in the dark with that one when her mama passed on. Michy was tiny, not a year old when her mama got sick," Walt said. "Old Greta helped me out, teaching the four of them their lessons." A chuckle rumbled from deep in his chest. "Couldn't figure out why the Big Guy had settled a Fulbright scholar smack in the middle of the desert till then—but I never doubted that He traveled in mysterious ways."

"Greta is a Fulbright scholar? *Greta* Greta? From the Hotel?"

"You bet," Walt said, nodding. He pulled a long cylindrical object from his breast pocket and bit off the end of it.

"Dad," Mich said, her voice a warning from the darkness that surrounded them.

"Hush now," he told his daughter gently. "May as well roll up now, if I can't enjoy a good smoke once in a while." He lit the end of the cigar and shook what was left of the match flame at Noah. "I figure there was only one thing I ever did that was truly wrong," he said, dropping the spent match in the dirt. "The worst thing I ever did was pretend she was a boy. Well, I didn't really pretend she was a boy, but I treated her like one. Treated them all the same." He paused.

"Dad," Mich said again.

"This one," he said, indicating Mich with the bright end of his cigar. "This one has the toughest character and the broadest stubborn streak of the lot. She's also the straightest thinker. Had all sorts of plans to go off to college once. She and old Greta did."

"But she had me instead," Eric said from the dirt, where he lay listening and looking at the stars. There was no shame in his voice, he was simply adding to the story as if it were one he'd heard a hundred times.

"She did indeed," Walt's voice boomed. "You know, Mr. Thomas . . ."

"Please. Call me, Noah." He just couldn't stand it any longer.

"Well, Noah, I never heard that saying everyone is spouting these days, the one about it taking a village to raise a child? But I think the Big Guy had that in mind for my family. And don't be thinking that I don't know this is a town full of misfits and oddballs, 'cause I do know it. The thing is, what's odder than a dumb trucker with nothing but a dream and a penny in his pocket trying to raise up four kids alone? Answer me that."

Falling in love with your nephew's mother? Lying to people you care about? Feeling as if you belong in a nowhere ghost town full of oddballs and misfits?

Noah could think of a great many things that were far stranger, but what he said was, "I don't know, sir. But I think you're right about the Big Guy moving in mysterious ways. Things seemed to have worked out very well for you."

"They have, indeed," Walt said, nodding his satisfaction, puffing on his cigar. "Even raising Mich up the way we did, she didn't turn out half-bad, don't you think?"

"Dad . . ."

Noah chuckled. "No, sir, not half-bad," he said, and he knew, even in the dark, that she was blushing.

He could easily imagine what it was like when they were all there, the brothers and Michelin and Walt and Eric, listening and watching the stars. He'd never known such envy or such a yearning before. The Albees were the family he'd always dreamed of—still dreamed of, night after night.

Images came to him clearly that night. Images of wrestling in new-mown grass with his nephew; a long walk on a sandy beach, barefoot, talking of nothing important with Walt; a long lazy afternoon with Mich in a hammock built for two, her dark eyes molten with passion; her lips wet, rosy, and freshly kissed; her body naked, warm, and tangled with his . . .

◆——◆——◆

He couldn't possibly have told her the truth that morning, he could barely look her in the eye with his dreams lingering in his mind.

"Well, actually, if you were serious about loaning me a truck, I think I'd like to drive out and see that lunar crater," he told her when she asked about his plans for the day, suggesting a ride on the horses before it got too hot. "Eric and I thought we'd go, if it was okay with you. Maybe we could go for that ride this evening?"

"Sure. Whenever," she said with a casual shrug, a sharp contradiction to the disappointment and confusion in her eyes. "Take the red one, it has air-conditioning. The keys are in it, and Eric knows the way to the crater."

It was all he could do to keep from calling her back, telling her the truth, and throwing himself on her mercy. But the dream was still so vivid in his mind. Her smell. Her heat. The sound of her voice in a passionate whisper . . .

"There's nothing to see out here," Eric told him a short time later in the cab of the truck. He'd been surprised by the invitation but glad of the reprieve from his morning lessons. "It's just a hole in the ground."

"Would you rather go to Duckwater, see the Indian reservation?"

"Not really. It's about as interesting as the crater." Eric watched his uncle with thoughtful eyes. "They have a pretty good trading post, though, if you're interested in that sort of thing."

"Not really," Noah said, flicking a quick glance at the boy. "What? I needed to get out of town, okay?"

"Is she getting to you?"

He frowned. "Who?" Eric's steady gaze told him they both knew who, but he wasn't prepared to discuss his emotions with a fourteen-year-old boy, particularly this fourteen-year-old boy. "What are you talking about?"

"You like her, don't you?" Eric persisted.

"What?" He *really* wasn't prepared for this.

"Are you falling in love with her?"

Noah sputtered stupidly, confirming, denying, and asserting total ignorance all at once.

"Would you be my dad, then, or still my uncle?"

Slamming on the brakes, Noah pulled the truck to the side of the road, turned to stare at Eric for a long minute, then lowered his head to the steering wheel with a heavy thunk.

He really truly wasn't prepared for any of this. Not for her. Not for the kid. Not for the feelings churning inside him. Lifting his head, he looked into the rearview mirror, into his own eyes, and wondered who he was looking at? A man who was honest and forthright? Or a liar? A man who was precise and trustworthy? Or a coward? His gaze shifted to Eric.

"Technically, I'd still be your uncle," he said, defeated.

Eric grinned, being privy to that confidence making him feel very grown up, and vastly enjoying the fact that his uncle was pinned between a rock and a hard place.

"Does she know yet?" he asked. "I mean, have you . . . you know . . ."

"No!" His face was fire hot, and he felt like a six-year-old caught with his hand in the cookie jar. "No.

There hasn't been any . . . you know." He hesitated. "But she might know."

"I think she likes you." Eric met his uncle's gaze straight on. "I've seen the way she looks at you."

Noah sighed, shook his head, and leaned back in the seat.

"I can't even kiss her until I tell her the truth," he said, glancing sideways to gauge the boy's reaction to this sort of talk.

Eric looked out the windshield, then turned his head to study the craggy peaks in the distance. He was quiet for so long that Noah began to feel that perhaps his feelings toward Michelin were something the boy might resent. She was his mother, after all. And he'd had her to himself all his life.

"Eric . . ."

"You should tell her, then," Eric said, speaking at the same time. "Soon. Just tell her and go on from there."

"Eric. How do you feel about all this? What do you think?"

As was his way, Eric lowered his gaze and considered his answer before speaking. "I don't know. I thought about it last night while I was watching her watch you. I know she's lonely sometimes."

"Do you . . . have any objections? To me? To . . . me and your mom?" There were three distinct questions in there somewhere.

Once again he was thoughtful.

"No. I don't think so."

Noah sighed his relief.

"Would we have to leave Gypsum?"

"I don't know. No. Not if you didn't want to."

They sat in the truck listening to a gentle breeze roll grains of sand across the desert floor. Noah envisioned the chaos and confusion the truth would ignite in Gypsum, Michelin's face when she heard it—and to a lesser extent, his own face once her brothers found out. He could see himself spending the rest of his life in exile from her, with no hope of ever seeing her smile again, of touching her. . . .

Eric, on the other hand, was envisioning something very different.

"What about babies?" the teenager asked abruptly.

"What?" It wasn't as if he needed the question repeated—it hung in the air like an anvil on a string. "Babies? Aren't you kind of jumping the gun here?"

"I think she wants more babies," he said soberly, watching Noah closely. "She told me once that she used to want a bunch of kids, but God sent her one special kid instead."

Noah nodded, sensing that his mother's happiness was a serious subject at the moment, that he was working the whole thing out in his mind before he gave his final seal of approval.

"I don't know about babies," Noah said honestly, feeling more like himself than he had in several days. "That's something we'd have to decide on later. You and me and your mom. I wouldn't mind having more kids around, if that's what you're asking. But I'd also be happy just being part of your life."

They observed each other for a full minute before Eric asked, "And what if she decides to hate you forever because of what happened before with my grandfather?

And because you didn't tell her the truth right off. What then?"

"You mean, what about us? You and me?" Noah gave a soft half laugh, amazed and deeply touched that the boy would worry about losing him. "It took me fourteen years to find you, to become an uncle. I like it. We'll figure out a way to stay in touch. Letters, phone calls . . . E-mail," he added brightly. "She might very well hate me, but she won't be afraid of me. She knows there's no way and nothing I can do to come between the two of you now. She won't keep us apart."

After that the trip to the crater seemed a waste of time. He'd firmly decided—and Eric was expecting it of him—to tell Michelin the truth as soon as possible.

But when they returned to town, hyped up and feeling incredibly brave between bouts of dread and panic, they discovered that Mich had left town in the opposite direction, toward Warm Springs, shortly after they'd left.

So, you see, he did have excuses to be sitting there, watching the sun set on yet another day of deception. Not that they made him feel any better about it, or that the additional time to contemplate the error of his ways had done anything but whittle away at his resolve.

A sincerely prudent and thrifty man would have been using this time to tell everyone else in Gypsum of his deception—Willa Shanks, Hank Meally, who owned the antique store in the Other Saloon, Art and Leslie Dunn, who ran the General Store, the Perkins family and Lester Funk, who delivered mail from one end of Nye County to the other—begging them all for their forgiveness. Practicing, as it were, for the ultimate test.

But self-preservation told him that if he saved his energy, took the biggest hurdle first and cleared it, the rest would be easier.

"No sense gluing your eyes to that window, boy." Walt's voice rattled against his eardrum, shattering his concentration. "She won't be here till she comes, you know."

He shifted his gaze from the sunset beyond the Saloon window and fixed it on the untouched beer in front of him. Walt had received word, once again, that his eldest son, Roy, wouldn't be making it back to town that night. Buck and Otis had both set out that morning on overnighters. So when Michelin didn't return by six o'clock, he'd invited Noah to take supper with him and Eric, insisting that while the cat was away, all the mice should play down at the Saloon.

Noah could have wished his thoughts weren't so obvious to everyone, but then, what difference did it make? They were all going to know the truth soon enough. He was crazy about Michelin, and he was liar.

He raised his eyes to the two men leaning on the bar beside and across from him. They looked back sympathetically.

"What?"

"Just getting one last good look at the man you were, boy." Walt shook his head and fought the grin trying to take over his mouth.

"The man I was?"

"If she hadn't taken ol' Greta with her, you might still be safe but . . ." Now Chuckie the bartender shook his head.

"Give me a break, will you?"

"I'm telling you," Chuckie said prophetically. "When two women from Gypsum travel all the way to Warm Springs to *shop*, they can only be buying one thing."

Noah suspected there were any number of things two women could buy in Warm Springs. It was certainly a larger town than Gypsum, with a greater variety of *shopping* possibilities. But Chuckie and Walt were both on their second beer and had, for some time now, been leading up to a point in their conversation.

"And what could that be?" Noah asked.

"A dress."

"A dress," he repeated, having expected something much more suggestive to go with the highly amused and meaningful twinkle in their eyes.

"A new dress," Walt repeated, barely able to control a teasing grin. "They don't go together to buy furniture. Or hardware. Or groceries. They only go together to buy new clothes. One buys the dress, and she takes the other one with her to ooh and ah. Definitely a new dress. And they've been gone long enough to get new underthings to go with it, so she feels pretty all the way down to her skin."

His gaze slid from one old face to the other and back again. He might have been surprised to hear a loving father speaking this way about his daughter, suggesting in tone and manner that his daughter's intentions were anything but pure and chaste. But this was Walt, who had already warned him that she had a broomstick logic no man could ignore, boasted that there was no one he'd rather have beside him in a brawl, and had proudly announced that she'd broken up more fights in that very saloon than Chuckie had in all the years he'd owned it. Hardly the sort of father who needed to worry about his daughter's virtue, he supposed.

He shrugged, refusing to play along with them.

"Michelin is pretty without clothes," Noah said simply. Both men burst out laughing. Turning red to the roots of his hair as he realized what he'd said, he quickly added, "What I meant was, she looks better without them." They laughed harder, turning the heads of the six other patrons in their direction. "She doesn't need a dress to be pretty."

Walt slammed an arm down on the bar and guffawed while Chuckie wiped away tears with his shirtsleeve.

"Oh, for Pete's sake."

Walt grabbed his shoulder and shook him back and forth on the bar stool. "Don't let us fluster you, boy. The night is just beginning. Once the girl gets here, you're gonna be plenty frustrated as it is."

"Oh, stop," he said, taking a long gulp of his beer. "Four beers between you, and you're drunk as two skunks in a trunk. You don't know she went specifically to buy a new dress. And even if she did, so what? Women buy new dresses all the time."

"Not Gypsum women," Walt said, still chuckling. "Gypsum women gotta have a good reason to buy a new dress. Something or *someone* special to wear it for."

"That's right," Chuckie joined in when he could.

"What do they need new dresses for out here in the middle of the nowhere? If not for something or *someone* special?"

He rolled his eyes and swiveled his stool around.

"Eric!" Noah called over the jukebox music. "Come beat the tar out of me at pool again, will you please?" If he were a lesser man, he might have thought himself the village kicking dog, glancing from the two highly amused old men to watch the way the boy's face lit up with the confidence of an easy win. If not for the friendship and affection in their eyes, he wouldn't have added, "You don't want to let these two old farts have all the fun, do ya?"

He was trying to stare down the killer look in Eric's eyes with a straight face as he walked toward him when, as if on cue, the final chord of the song on the jukebox slowly faded out and two shapely legs appeared below the swinging doors of the Saloon.

He was never sure if he looked first or simply followed everyone else's gaze to the doors, but when they swung open to let Michelin in, he would always remember the thunder roaring inside his head and the way he wobbled unsteadily when the earth rolled and shook beneath him.

His mouth went instantly dry at the sight of her in a simple classic black dress with tiny strings across the shoulders and a full, flowing skirt that hit her midthigh, her long, sexy legs encased in sheer black silk. Her dark hair tumbled in soft loose curls to her bare shoulders, her skin glowing as if kissed by the sun.

His heart was beating wildly in his chest. He wasn't

at all sure he was even breathing. He tried to swallow and made such a loud, strangled noise that Chuckie had to turn around and check stock while Walt held his beer to his lips and let his shoulders vibrate with silent laughter.

SEVEN

Mich wasn't above changing her clothes to demonstrate that she was as much woman as she was a tow-truck driver, mechanic, chief cook and bottle washer, arm wrestler, and single mother of a teenager. She was a strong, confident, self-reliant woman with too much self-respect ever to use obvious, explicit sexual overtures to get what she wanted . . . unless it was absolutely necessary.

She had no idea what was keeping Noah at arm's length from her, but she was certain it wasn't what either of them wanted.

Not when the air seemed to sizzle when they came into each other's company, deliberately or by accident. Not when they seemed to be constantly touching, by mishap or design. Not when she'd catch him watching her, dreamy-eyed, or when she couldn't gather two thoughts around his constant presence in her mind.

No, tonight she was a powerful woman with hidden skills and secret talents. An exorcist, determined to drive out—or at least find out about—whatever it was that kept pulling at him, tugging him away from her.

She had a bevy of butterflies in her belly as she stood there, screwing up her courage to go get what she wanted. She couldn't be wrong about him. She wouldn't be able to feel the honesty and goodness in him if it wasn't there, would she? Why would she ache for him if he had nothing with which to ease her pain?

She pushed the swinging doors of the Saloon wide open and stepped inside, meeting his gaze almost immediately.

He stood staring at her, stunned, as if she'd suddenly stabbed him without provocation. Her heart fluttered and skipped about in her chest, her breath came fast and shallow.

She had his attention now, by golly. Someone young and careless giggled inside her. The black silk of the dress skimmed against her naked skin, cool and smooth, arousing feminine charms she'd almost forgotten she had. She felt sexy. Magical.

A bar stool squeaked loudly in the silence that followed her entrance. Her gaze gravitated slowly to her father, who had turned to admire her openly, with his big arms crossed in satisfaction across his midsection. His eyes twinkled at her with pride and good humor, as they had most every day that she could remember. A slim smile and an encouraging wink from him was all it took to top off her tank of resolve.

She took aim at her target and started walking toward him. He could have been dead and nailed upright to the floor for all she knew, standing there motionless, staring, his expression one of dumb wonder.

But the closer she got, the clearer she could see his chest rising and falling as he took deep bracing breaths, the difficulty he had swallowing, and a barely perceivable, very endearing, trembling of his hands.

In the back of her brain she registered Eric's enthusiastic voice, but not what he was saying. His presence played on the lacy fringes of her mind, slowly working its way to the foreground, so that by the time she was to toe-to-toe with Noah, she'd come to a conclusion about it.

"It's time to go to bed," she said.

"Wh-what?" Noah asked, turning very pale.

"Awww, Mom," Eric groused, having recognized her *mother* tone of voice. "One more game of pool, okay? I—"

"Now please," she said, cutting him off, her gaze never leaving Noah's face.

There was an irritating buzzing in his ears, but what she was saying was coming through loud and clear. It was time they went to bed. Yes, he agreed. Definitely. No problem. He even worked his mouth to tell her as much, but no sound came out. The buzzing got louder.

"Man, this is so unfair," Eric complained. "Anytime anything fun happens around this place, I have to leave. Go to bed, Eric. Go do your studies, Eric. Feed the horses, Eric. Clean your room. Go check on Greta. Go help Max, Eric. It's not fair. I'm old enough—"

"Eric," Noah said, discovering the source of the buzz and seeing confusion and frustration in the boy's face. He picked a quarter out of his pocket and flipped it high into the air across the room. Eric caught it instinctively. "Pick out a good song on that thing." He motioned to the jukebox with his head, then looked back at Michelin, adding, "A long, slow one. And then get lost, will you?"

It was the divergence between the gentle tone of voice and the rudeness of the words that had Eric taking a new look at the situation. His "Oh. Oooooh!" made Noah smile.

Mich smiled back, grateful she wouldn't have to scream like a banshee at her son and spoil the illusion she'd gone to so much trouble to create. She was delighted when Noah's hand slipped around hers and she felt his other hand at her waist, drawing her into his arms.

When the music started, it startled them both, and Noah glanced over her shoulder to see that the bar had been cleared, and Walt and Eric were standing beside the door preparing to leave too. He winked at his nephew and smiled, and received a conspirator's grin in return.

"They've all gone home," he said, feeling stiff-jointed and awkward despite the fact that they were merely swaying together in time to some sad old western tune he didn't know. "Everyone in town seems to know what's happening here except me."

Mich smiled a smile that would have warned him of great danger if he hadn't been caught and drowning in the depths of her dark eyes.

"I think you know what's happening."

Okay, he did. But he needed to talk off the nervous energy building up inside him. He needed to tell her something important. He just couldn't recall what.

"Mich, we need to talk," he said, his voice low and

soft, chasing shivers up her spine. "I . . . I have a confession to make."

"I know," she said, trying not to smile.

"You do?"

Her eyes were twinkling with good humor, which confused him. If she knew what he was about to say and thought it amusing, he was home free! He could pull her close and kiss her mindless. He could relish the feel of her skin against his. Tell her *everything, anything*. All about his life, his dreams, his worries. They could get married. Live happily ever after and—

"Yes," she was saying, giddy with anticipation. "I found the rags in your exhaust pipe this morning."

"My . . . the what?"

"The rags? Stuffed up the tailpipe of your car? Familiar-looking rags, no less, which means you put them there *after* I towed you back here."

"The rags?"

"The rags that were choking the engine. That you put there. So you could stay here longer."

His face was so hot, he feared his head was steaming. Any second now he expected spontaneous combustion to occur, and he'd disappear in a cloud of black smoke.

No such luck.

"Michelin, I'm sorry about that. I . . ."

She started to laugh. She rested her forehead on his chest briefly, then raised it again to look at him.

"I jammed the valves in your distributor."

"You . . ." He grinned, chuckled softly. "So I'd have to stay."

She nodded without remorse. "I could have fixed it quickly enough if you'd wanted to leave, but you didn't seem to mind being here, and I . . . I didn't mind having you here."

They didn't really need to talk anymore. No more wondering. No more games. They were falling in love. They wanted each other, needed to be with each other, belonged together.

They stood together, touching lightly, pretending to dance. The music drifted away, and in the silence they pondered the vastness of what they'd been trying to control. Another song started up, but they hardly noticed. Nothing and no one but the two of them existed. Their world became a space two feet square, massive in its intensity, crowded with emotions, profuse with desire.

They came to a gradual standstill, connected by touch and thought.

"I fixed your distributor three days ago," she murmured faintly, offering him his freedom to leave but making it sound exactly like *I love you*. He didn't speak, but the gentleness and profound passion he was feeling was plain in his expression. "Do you . . . ? Will you . . . ? Please, kiss me."

He could hardly breathe. She was so beautiful, so much of what his dreams had become. Just once, he thought, watching her eyes grow dark with longing as he leaned toward her. Just one kiss, he told himself, pushing guilt and regret to the back of his mind as her eyes slowly closed and their lips brushed. *One* was his last thought as he covered her mouth with his, wedged his tongue between her teeth, and tasted her until he could neither think nor stop himself from taking more.

Her breath escaped her when he crushed her in his

embrace. Her heart hammered fire-hot blood through her veins as her senses exploded, scattering fragments of delight and joy and excruciating need to the stars and beyond. She clung to him, bunching his shirt in her hands, tasting and teasing. Longing gnawed at her.

To hell with it, he decided in the weakest moment of his life. He could be Noah Thomas for ever. Who'd care? Who'd know the difference? Who'd risk giving all this up for the truth? he wondered, filling his hands with her hair, taking in the scent of her, devouring the softness of her throat with his lips.

She shattered when she felt his hand on her breast, instinctively pressing herself closer to that spot that was both pain and ecstasy. Pulling his shirt from his waistband, her fingers tingled against smooth warm skin, felt muscles quiver for control.

"Michelin," he whispered, his voice groggy and hoarse. "Oh, Mich."

"Please," she said, her lips against his. "Let's go to your room. Make love to me."

Desperately, he continued to kiss her, to battle off rational thought, to keep the truth at bay.

"Noah. Please," she said, growing weak-kneed, her nerves in an overstimulated frenzy. Dragging him to the floor of the Saloon was fast becoming a viable solution to her distress.

And so it was with great surprise and a massive shock to her various life-support systems that she became aware that Noah had suddenly pushed her away and was standing a good six feet from her.

"Oh. What have I done? God, what have I done?"

he kept muttering as the room spun slowly back into focus, the jukebox spinning the Platters' "Only You."

"What?" she asked, confused and frightened, dreading the moment she'd come here for, that she'd set out to create. She'd make him tell her, she had to know, but would she be as happy then as she had been a moment ago? "Tell me," she said, before she changed her mind.

He pleaded for understanding with his eyes. "My name is Tessler."

"What?"

"My name is Noah Thomas Tessler . . ." he said, his voice trailing off as he realized she'd understood him the first time and that *what* was simply the beginning of a hundred questions skittering through her head. What are you doing here? What do you want? What's the big idea of coming in here under an assumed name? What do you think you're doing, kissing me with your filthy lying mouth? "Mich, I—"

"How dare you?" she asked. Clearly having drawn her own conclusions to the *what*s, she was now starting in on the *how*s. "How could you do this?"

"Michelin, please, let me explain. It's not what you think."

"How do you know what I think? You know nothing about me."

"Yes, I do," he said, taking a step toward her, only to have her back away, tears shimmering in her lovely eyes. "I know all about you. And Eric. And Walt. And my brother. That's why I came here."

"To weasel yourself in here and to let us trust you and talk to you and treat you like a friend? Why? Why now? You must know Eric won't go with you. Go ahead, offer to give him anything he wants, he's too smart to fall for that. He won't go with you."

"I didn't come here for Eric."

"Why then? To completely destroy every happy memory I ever had of being with a man I loved? To humiliate me? Why would you do that? Where will this get you? Eric *loved* you. When did you become such a hateful person? When will you Tesslers leave me *alone*?"

What, who, why, where, when . . . that covered all the questions. Now it was his turn to talk.

"Oh! Eric," she said before he could open his mouth, a new surge of anger sweeping across her features. "What about Eric? He likes you. He trusts you. You hurt my son, and so help me I'll—"

"Stop it," he said, not shouting but in a voice loud enough to get through to her. "Eric knows."

"He knows?"

"He figured it out the day I arrived. From some pictures in your closet. I half suspect your father knows, too, but he hasn't said anything."

Having to have the obvious pointed out to her made her even angrier. Looking at him now, she could see the resemblance around the eyes and mouth, had seen it all along, she supposed, but hadn't made the connection.

"Well, isn't that just great? Sneaking in here under an assumed name, conspiring behind my back with my son, sucking up to my dad and my brothers—"

"Falling in love with you . . ." he said, tacking his biggest crime to the tail of her sentence.

"Love? Love? You're a Tessler. What do you know about love?" she said, intentionally trying to hurt him.

"Not much," he admitted. But he knew enough that

to see her in such pain was tearing him apart, to know she felt betrayed filled him with shame, to feel her outrage was frightening beyond anything he'd known before. "I didn't mean for it to happen. I didn't mean for any of this to happen. I never intended for it to go this far, or for so long. It just . . . happened. I came here to meet you. That's all. I only wanted to meet you, under normal circumstances, not as the long-lost uncle and brother-in-law. I didn't even know about you until—"

"Is that the way you high-society people do things? You come to meet someone and give them a fake name, pretend to be someone else?"

"No. That . . . that part was stupid. It was a mistake. I know that now. I was trying to make it easier on everyone, lessen the shock of it. I was wrong. I'm sorry." He took an involuntary step forward and once again felt a stab of pain through his heart when she backed away from him. "Mich, I made a mistake. I swear to God, I never intended to hurt you or to lure Eric away from you or to show any disrespect to your family. I just wanted to know you. All of you."

"I, I, I," she said, ignoring the places in her heart that were weakening with love and understanding. "That's such a typically Tessler response to everything. I thought, I meant, I wanted . . . never a thought to what other people are thinking and wanting."

"Will you give me a break here?" he asked, frustrated by her angry refusal to hear anything he was saying. "The only thing I lied about was my name, and I apologized for that. The rest of it, everything else, is true."

"And you think apologizing makes everything fair and square between us." It was a statement that made *him* sound naive.

"No. But I think it's a place to start. We could begin again. You could give me another chance. If you'd let me, I could prove to you that your instincts about me were right, that I'm someone you can trust . . . and care about."

"Hmmph." A disbelieving snort. She glanced away, then back in a flash. "Why should I? Give you another chance. Why should I?"

Because if she didn't, he'd wither, dry up, and blow away. He was certain of it.

"Because . . ."

"That's not an answer," she said, without letting him finish.

"Because," he repeated patiently, "I'm Eric's uncle and I don't want to lose him. Because I am your friend, whether you believe me right now or not. And because I've fallen in love with you and need a chance to prove myself to you."

She didn't want to believe him, didn't want to give him a second chance. But his words were so true, they were nearly palpable. Could have been etched in stone. And the simple fact was . . . she loved him too.

"Listen to me," he said gently when she couldn't think of anything appropriate to say, anything that would satisfy both her anger and her affection. He took a step closer and, when she didn't back away, took another. He reached out to touch her.

"Don't even think of touching me," she said with a

growl. Her hormones were out of their box and still extremely unpredictable. His hands fell to his sides.

"I know you're angry. I knew you would be. And you have a right to be. But we don't have to throw it all away on one admittedly stupid mistake." He hesitated. "I don't expect you to feel the same way about me. Now probably wouldn't be a good time for this," he said, looking down at her in the clinging black silk, sighing heavily. "But . . . but we can be friends. Become better friends, and then maybe later . . ."

"Friends?" she asked, as if it were something as incredible as a pig laying eggs, as rare as a winged cat, as unlikely as a fundamentalist with a sense of humor. "Friends? Are you out of your mind?"

"No," he said, taking her confusion as a chink in her armor. In his best diplomatic manner, he laid out his arbitration plan. "We'll start now, being open and completely honest with each other. No more secrets. We can talk, share our interests and our thoughts, do things together." She shot him a contemptuous look. "Like go bowling or to a rodeo or—"

"Like old pals? Buddies?" she said, formulating a plan of her own. "We can say anything that's on our minds? Ask favors of each other? Learn to count on each other?"

"Yes, exactly." He smiled, congratulating himself on falling in love with a wonderfully tolerant and loving woman. He realized it would take some time to win back her trust, but that she was giving him a chance was all he could ask for at the moment.

"And it would be platonic, right? No, ah, you know . . ."

"Absolutely," he said, grateful for any crumb that fell from the table.

"Except, maybe later, then we could . . . maybe."

"Yes," he said, his spirits soaring. On that hope alone, he could wait till Judgment Day. "Definitely. When you're ready we can . . . you know, maybe try this again."

He *was* out of his mind, she decided, glancing away before she started to laugh. If he truly believed they could be anything less than the most intimate of lovers, that the bond between them wasn't just as physical as it was emotional, intellectual, and spiritual—he'd clearly gone round the bend.

"And this friendship would begin now?" she asked, as if considering his proposal.

"Right now, this second."

"And you won't ever lie to me again?"

"On my honor, I swear."

"All right," she said, agreeing to nothing. "Why didn't you come sooner? Why did you wait all these years?"

All those wasted years.

A brief, relieved laugh escaped him. "I didn't even know you existed until six weeks ago. I . . ." He frowned. "I should have guessed, maybe. Eric wrote to me about you before he died. Told me he was in love with this girl he'd met, but he didn't mention marriage. I didn't know he'd planned to marry you or about the boy until . . ." He hesitated. "Mich, my father passed away about two months ago."

He waited for a joyful hoot, but instead she was quiet and introspective, lowering her eyes to the floor.

"I can't say I'm sorry, but you must have been close to him, so I—"

"I wasn't," he said. "He wasn't an easy man to get close to." He followed her to a table and took the chair across from her. "You see, Eric and I didn't grow up together. I was away at school most the time. But we cared about each other, loved each other. And I didn't abandon my brother." She met his gaze. "We'd talked about my leaving. He knew what I wanted to be, what I wanted to do with my life. I'd spent my whole life preparing for what I do now. I was twenty-six years old. I'd put in my time as an aide to Senator Partlow and as an aide in the American embassy in Great Britain, then later as an adjunct to Philip Cresten, ambassador to Angola. But Eric . . . he . . . well, when I was offered jobs that involved more responsibility, I didn't feel like I could take them. Not while he was still in school. I knew Eric still needed me, he . . . well, like you said, he got into trouble a lot. I'd taken a desk job in Washington, nothing special, nothing I really wanted to do. But I could call in sick for a few days while I helped him out of whatever fix he'd gotten himself into, and no one cared or noticed too much. It was my best bet, at least until he finished school."

She said nothing.

"My father . . ." He looked away to conceal the bitterness he felt then gave a short laugh. "I was more of a father to Eric than a brother really, certainly more so than our father was. You wouldn't believe how often I heard him say, 'He made his bed, now let him lie in it.' The man was hard. A hard man. And spending time in jail wasn't what Eric needed."

"So you helped him."

"As much as I could. I was almost eight years older, the only adult who ever showed up and was willing to post bail for him, but I wasn't enough. He needed to feel he belonged, that he was wanted. He needed a real family."

"Like mine."

His smile was small but perceptive. "Just like yours."

They were both quiet, picturing Eric, wallowing in the love the Albees radiated, constantly and unconsciously.

"We had a deal," he said at last. "A temporary position—ten months, twelve at the most—as roving ambassador to a newly established democratic government in a small country in Africa came up, and I wanted it. Badly. I needed it to get my career off the ground. But I was afraid Eric would do something and I'd have to come back before I'd built up a good rapport with the new leaders, and . . . Well, I called Eric at school and told him about it and what I was worried about and . . ."

His voice faded away, and he closed his eyes on the memory.

"And he promised to be a good boy until you got back?" she asked, aware that his pain was still as fresh and raw as it had been fifteen years before, that he hadn't resolved any of the issues he and Eric had left in the air. He nodded. "Did you know he'd left school?" He shook his head. "But you knew about me?"

"He wrote. Letters. He'd never done that before. Usually it was a phone call in the middle of the night."

He paused. "That alone should have made me suspicious. He could almost as easily have called. But I was always so glad to get his letters. It never occurred to me. I didn't even look at the cancellations on the envelopes until after I'd been notified of his death."

"So you thought I was some girl he'd met at school." He nodded, glancing at her briefly. "And you never knew about his son?"

He shook his head and sighed.

"There were letters in my father's effects. One from Eric, and yours informing him of Eric's birth. He never told me. And I never dreamed . . ."

"And that was six weeks ago."

"About that . . ." He leaned back in the chair, nodding, the most difficult part of the story told—and somehow easier to bear. "I didn't know what to do at first. Leave well enough alone or try to contact you through the mail? But I wanted to meet you. See Eric. I . . . had you investigated," he said, blurting out the words, knowing the thin ice he was skating on could crack and split wide open at any moment.

"Investigated?" She actually laughed. "I bet that was a dull report."

"It was. Not even a speeding ticket."

"And nothing about the custody hearings?"

"No," he said as a rush of guilt swept over him. The sins of the father, he supposed. "And there was nothing about it in my father's papers. That was a surprise to me too."

"Why? Because he wasn't the best of fathers the first time around, so why would he want to try it again with a grandson?"

He nodded. "There's one more thing you should probably know about."

She looked at him, waiting. Unlike him, nothing about his father could surprise her. She'd spent the last fourteen years of her life trying to outthink and outmaneuver the man's wickedness, based nearly all her decisions on what he might or might not do—whether he was really out there watching or not.

"You remember when we first met I told you I was here on personal business and business-business?"

"Yes."

"Obviously, meeting you and Eric was the personal business, but I also came to tell you that you're rich."

"What?"

"Rich." A pause. "You and Eric have inherited a great deal of money from my father's estate."

"He left us money?" She couldn't have been more surprised if he'd gut-punched her. And then it occurred to her. "If he left us money . . . but you didn't find out about us until you went through his things . . . ?"

"He didn't exactly leave it to you," he said slowly. So slowly, each word sank into her mind as he said it.

"He left it all to you. And you feel guilty about it. So you're giving some to us," she guessed, her temper rising like steam in a pressure cooker.

"No," he said quickly, recognizing the look in her eyes from a short time earlier. "No. It's not like that. I don't feel guilty. I have nothing to feel guilty about. It's yours by right. Eric would have received half if he'd lived, his wife and child if they survived him. It's your money. It was decided the moment I found out about you, before I came to meet you."

"I don't want it. We weren't married."

"You were as good as married. And you had his son."

"It's not legal. You can't make me take it," she said impulsively.

"Mich! For crying out loud, can you hear yourself talking? We're talking about a great deal of money here. Enough money to send Eric to school. Enough to buy him his own college. A small, private, unknown college, maybe . . . But think about it before you stick that stubborn chin out at me and tell me you won't take it."

He stopped short to take a new approach. "Look. I can understand that you wouldn't want to take anything that ever belonged to my father, as a matter of pride. But it never really belonged to him. Not the bulk of it, anyway. My parents' marriage was more like a merger. My father's powerful old name and a fortune my mother's family made in telecommunications after World War Two. The Tesslers were nearly broke. So you see, the money was really my mother's, and would have gone to Eric if he'd lived."

"But he didn't," she said, her voice echoing loudly through the empty bar room, the jukebox now flashing soundlessly. "And he didn't marry me, and his son is an Albee. But more importantly, we don't need the money. I've seen what money can do to people. And we're doing just fine without it."

"Right. You're arm-wrestling for Eric's education."

"What's wrong with that?" Her chin and her nose both went in the air. "It's honest. It's fair. And if I lose —and I'm not planning to—I can always take out a loan on Dad's trucking company."

"That's ridiculous. Why would you do all that when you've got a fortune sitting in the bank waiting to be spent?"

"Because I *don't* have a fortune in the bank," she said, standing. "And I don't want it. You keep it."

"I don't want it either," he said, standing to have a face-off. "I already have one. This one belongs to you."

"No, it doesn't."

"Yes. It does."

"Give it to charity, then."

"Are you crazy?"

"Let me think about it," she said cautiously. "Maybe a trust fund for Eric wouldn't be such a bad thing."

"Whatever you think is best," he said, working hard on his bland expression as he watched her eyes light up with possibilities.

"But he's still my child, and I'll raise him the way I see fit," she said.

"Absolutely."

"And his education is my responsibility. I'm still going to the competition. I'm going to win and Eric is going to a real school."

"If that's the way you want it."

But it wasn't the way she wanted it. She opened her mouth to tell him so, then realized she already had.

"That's the way it has to be," she said, feeling suddenly drained and empty. This wasn't the evening she'd planned to have. Being suddenly rich was overwhelming, to say the least. Add to that the relief of knowing that Noah's hesitation had been caused by something as simple as a lie, and she was as near numb as she ever hoped to be.

"You have any more little revelations for me?" she asked, preparing to leave.

"No. I think that's about it," he said, wishing there was something he could do or say that would put the spark back in her eyes, to make her smile.

"Good. No more surprises," she said, walking away. "I really hate surprises. Good night."

"Michelin?" he said, waiting for her to turn back to him. "Friends, right?"

He looked so unsure, and even a little frightened, that she was tempted to smile and put him at ease. Instead, she gave him a good hard look and said, "We'll see."

EIGHT

"We're in the money. Ho-ha-la-la-la." Bright sunny days were a dime a dozen in Gypsum, but this one was *that* much brighter, *that* much sunnier as to put a bounce in Mich's step and a song in her heart. "We're in the money. Ho-ha-la-la-la."

She pulled the door to Eddy's wide and sashayed in. She smiled at neighbors, waved to a couple of trucker acquaintances, and called a good morning through the window to Max.

"Great day, huh?" she asked Noah, sliding her backside down the back of the booth to sit across from him.

"It is now," he said, grinning, encouraged by the bright look in her eyes. He watched her reach across the table to take one of the two bacon strips from his breakfast plate, tear it in half, and pop one end in her mouth, depositing the other back on his plate.

"Mmmm . . . Max has a way with bacon," she said, then took several long gulps of his orange juice. "Crispy-chewy, just right."

"Would like some of your own?" he asked, unaccustomed to other people eating off his plate. "Are you hungry? Can I buy you breakfast."

"No, thanks. I ate already." She removed the other half strip of bacon from his plate and ate it. "I've been giving some thought to your suggestion—the one about us being friends?"

He nodded, holding his breath.

"And I think we should give it a try. For Eric's sake. You are, after all, his uncle, and I can't remember the last time I enjoyed someone's company as much as yours. I think we could be good friends. Real pals."

"You do?" he asked, feeling a distinct disappointment. She'd given him the words he'd hoped to hear, but they were somehow missing something. "Good," he said, watching the last of his bacon being divided and partially consumed. He took up his coffee and held it protectively in both hands. "I'm glad. I think we—"

"And I'll take the money too," she said, all business. "In trust for Eric."

"I think that's a wise decision. I can—"

"You planning to go to Flagstaff with me?" she asked, cutting him off as she finished the orange juice and set the empty glass on the table.

"Ah. Yes. I'd like to. If you don't mind."

She reached across the table and took the last half sliver of bacon from his plate and popped it in her mouth. "Why would I mind? I'm driving, so if you want to go with me, we can split the gas."

"Well, fine. That'll be fine. Good. And we leave tomorrow, right?"

She nodded, reaching for a triangle of whole-wheat

toast. "It's a little over three hundred miles, so we can do it two ways," she said, slathering grape jelly on his toast. "Take turns driving and drive straight through. Or take the camper, take our time, camp out overnight. It doesn't matter to me as long as I'm there by Thursday afternoon for weigh-ins."

Time alone with her was what he wanted.

"Well, since I'm a tourist, let's take our time. I wouldn't mind seeing more of the country."

She nodded, licking grape jelly off her lips.

He watched her lick the jelly off her fingers, her tongue lithe and pink and wet. Her lips full and rosy. Her eyes dark, their expression concealed behind a fan of dark lashes.

"Are you sure you wouldn't like me to order you your own plate of food?"

"No, no. I just wanted a little taste. So, are you planning to wear those clothes in Flagstaff too?"

Noah looked down at his khaki slacks and respectable cotton knit shirt, then back at Mich, askance.

"Well, it's just that they look as out of place as a milk bucket under a bull, is all. 'Course, if you don't mind looking like a tourist . . . I just thought I'd help you pick out some different clothes—if you were feeling awkward in those, that is."

Awkward? Well, he sure as hell felt awkward in them now.

"You're kidding, right?" he asked a short time later, waddling stiff-legged from behind the curtained dressing room of Willa Shanks's bathhouse-turned-clothing-store. They could have painted the thick stiff denim on his legs and not gotten a tighter fit. "I can't even bend my knees."

"They'll bag out the longer you wear them," she told him, glancing at him briefly, then turning away to hide her expression. "Do you want snaps or buttons on your shirts?"

She was enthusiastically checking the sizes of a rack of men's shirts, scrutinizing colors and workmanship, carefully pondering the style. She was so clearly eager to make him feel as if he fit in and belonged. His heart warmed and sent a soothing heat throughout his chest.

"What about some stonewashed or at least prewashed jeans? Maybe a little wider leg? These are like ballet tights."

"Ballet tights?" she asked, giving him a silly look. "You want critters crawling up your legs? Those'll fit down snug over a pair of boots, unless you're planning to wear sneakers?"

He could tell by her tone that soft-soled shoes of any kind were as namby-pamby as taking stuffed toys to bed.

"So . . . cowboys boots, you think?" he asked.

"Or loggers. Or high-top hiking boots, if you feel like making a fashion statement."

"All right, cowboy boots," he said, resigned. Walt and the boys wore them, he supposed he could too. "But no weird animals' skins. No shiny pointed toes. And just medium-high heels."

In the end he finally had to insist on what she called a "dung"-colored cotton shirt and a "ratty"-looking hat with a simple leather band, but he did give in on her choice for his final purchase—but then, how far wrong could he go with a simple "USA" on his big silver belt buckle?

And to tell you the truth, once Willa secretly passed him a slightly larger pair of jeans, he didn't think he looked half-bad.

"So? What do you think?" he asked both ladies, presenting himself for a final inspection. "Do I look corn-fed and raised on country air?"

"You do, indeed," Willa said, clasping her hands under her small breasts, nodding repeatedly. "You're a fine figure of a man. Very handsome."

"He's already decided to buy the stuff, Willa. Let's not go overboard. Let's just say he looks better than he did before and leave it at that," Mich said, barely looking at him. In fact, looking a bit ill.

"Are you all right?" he asked, concerned, even as he stung from her remark.

"Yes. Sure." She was looking at some point on the wall directly over his left shoulder. "Nice duds. You ready to go? I've got things to do."

"Yep, all set." He thanked Willa for her help with a meaningful look, then followed Mich out the door. "Can I help you with anything? Got anything I can muck out for ya?"

She laughed, though he could tell she didn't want to.

"You aren't going to start talking like John Wayne now, are you?"

"Well, I don't know about that, little lady," he mimicked, strutting up close to her. "How good are you at playing Maureen O'Hara?"

She stepped back, and he smiled when she got big-eyed and swallowed hard.

"Not . . . not good. I don't play anyone but Mich Albee."

"Well, little missy," he said, closing the space between them again, putting his hands on her hips. She trembled, and springtime bloomed inside of him. "That's even better."

"Hey!" she cried, pushing his hands away. "None of that."

"But you like that," he said, still close but not touching her. "I can tell."

"Maybe I do. But friends don't do that."

"Do what?"

"You know, get close . . . in each other's faces. Touch. Try to kiss each other."

"I didn't try to kiss you."

"You didn't?"

His grin broadened and he shook his head slowly.

"Oh. Well good. Because that's not the kind of friendship we're going to have."

"Just yet."

"We'll see." She backed away from him, holding one hand out to keep him from following. "We'll see."

He hung his thumbs in his new pockets and leaned back on his new heels with a smirk on his face as he watched her walk back to the garage.

Okay, so he was more confused than annoyed when she ate off his plate. And okay, he looked fantastic in jeans and his shoulders seemed twice as wide in plaid and he was born to wear a Stetson, the brim shading his eyes, making them darker, keener, and somehow mysterious. So . . . okay. She wasn't done yet. She'd only just begun, in fact.

It wasn't that she was even angry anymore. Part of her understood his reluctance to walk cold into Eric's life after so many years of silence, understood the circumstances that led him to his decision. But dammit, he was a Tessler. Not a reckless, self-pitying youth or a mean, hurtful old man. A responsible family member who was going to have to bear the brunt of the frustrated emotions that had built up during her long love-hate relationship with his kinsman—whether or not it was fair or even rational on her part.

She was also willing to admit to the possibility that she might be angry that it was so easy for her to fall in love with another Tessler. What was it about the two brothers that attracted her? They were so different, and yet so intrinsically alike in some way, that she was attracted to them like someone drawn to the sight of a burning building.

"You're not much of a morning person, I take it," he said, his voice as close to her as his image in her mind.

She looked at him, sitting across the cab of the truck, and felt a longing unlike any she'd known before —then purposefully squelched it. They'd left Gypsum shortly after sunup and traveled nearly an hour, saying very little.

"I like to be where I'm going," she said, watching the road diligently, though there was little traffic.

"What else do you like?"

"What?"

"Tell me what else you like. Give me list. It's like counting sheep, it'll make the trip faster."

She gave him a blank look, weighing the value of his suggestion to her general plan. She must have looked confused, because he said, "Do you like ice cream?"

"Yes."

"What flavor?"

"Chocolate."

"See. It's easy. Now, what's your favorite time of day?"

"Dawn."

"Why?"

"I like the colors of it, and the newness of it. It's fresh. Full of potential . . . and possibilities. And it's quiet."

"You like that it's quiet?"

"Yeah." She glanced at his puzzled expression. "Well, wouldn't you think that something as huge and magnificent and absolutely necessary as the sun would, I don't know, make a lot more noise when it showed up? Bells and sirens, or maybe a loud crackling noise? But no, it just rises slowly in the sky, shines its warmth and light on everything, day after day. Quietly."

He leaned closer to her. "Tell me what you think of the moon."

"No. Not if you're going to make fun of me."

"I'm not. I swear. Tell me."

"I think . . . sometimes, that the moon is . . . shy."

"Shy," he said, tumbling the word around in his mind. "Because most of the time it hides from the sun, letting the earth take all its light and warmth. But when the earth moves away, and it gets the sun's full attention, it shines."

She wagged her head back and forth. "Yeah, sort of . . ."

"And the stars? Tell me about the stars."

This went on for some time. The subjects ranging from favorite holidays to her opinions on the most humanlike animals—a toss-up between monkeys and dolphins. And each time she was reluctant to speak, he scooted closer to her on the seat, to encourage her, until finally he was close enough to touch.

"I know that," she said, backhanding him in the chest and laughing. He caught her hand and held it lightly in his. Goose bumps marched up her arm and down her spine, and she looked at him. He was studying her fingers. "You asked for favorite fruits and vegetables, and, ah, just because I listed tomatoes with the vegetables that doesn't mean I, um, don't know it's a fruit."

"My grandmother would sometimes serve fried green tomatoes for lunch when we visited . . . because my mother liked them," he said, as if lost in a dream. "My father would refuse to sit at the table because the taste of them was intolerable and the sight of them reminded him of my mother's roots."

"He said that?" she asked softly, appalled. "Out loud? To your mother? And your grandmother?"

"Every time fried green tomatoes were served," he said, looking at her. "I told you he was hard."

"Hmmph," she snorted, angry. "That's not the word I'd use for that sort of behavior."

He chuckled and smoothed the skin on the back of her hand.

"No. I'm sure it isn't, but we won't go there. Okay, you know tomatoes are a fruit and anything with rice in it is out, because rice reminds you of maggots. We know you like sex, so let's move along to old movies. Do you have a favorite?"

"Ah . . . Wait a second. *We* don't know that I like sex."

"Sure we do," he said, brushing a finger along the soft sensitive skin on the underside of her arm. "*Casablanca*, right?"

"No, that's not my favorite." She snatched her arm away, bearing down on an urge to shake the fire off. "And how do *we* know I like sex?"

He chuckled. "You're not exactly a subtle woman, Michelin."

"I . . . What's that supposed to mean?"

"It means," he said, in a voice spilling seduction like a too-full teacup, "that every time I get this close to you, your eyes get a little darker, almost black, very mysterious. Your breath comes a little faster." He ran the back of his index finger down the column of her neck to the pulse skipping along at the bottom of it. "Your heart beats a little faster, and your skin gets warmer."

"Stop that! I'm driving. And you're dead wrong. I feel fine." A quick eye to the speedometer and she took her foot off the gas to slow everything down.

"You do, indeed," he said, sliding his finger back up her neck, under her chin, and across her lower lip. Her fingers turned white as she gripped the steering wheel.

"So soft. Warm. Very fine." The back of his hand brushed against her cheek, pushing her hair away from her face, exposing her ear. "Irresistible. You're incredibly beautiful too."

She felt his breath on her neck and held hers. She felt his lips skim her ear, and her eyelids grew heavy. Shivers of delight skipped across her body.

"You'd better stop that," she muttered, but even to her own ears it sounded remarkably like *more, more, more, more*.

"Mmm . . . You smell so good." He nibbled at her earlobe, his hand on her midsection, just below her breasts. Excitement engulfed her. Desire stirred lower in her abdomen.

"Noah," she whispered, the road blurring in front of her. On instinct alone, her foot moved to the brake and pressed lightly, slowing the truck to a crawl. She felt his hand cover hers on the steering wheel when she turned her face to his, felt the pull, knew they were leaving the highway. His mouth covered hers, and she punched the brake to the floor, heard the transmission click into park, and let go of the wheel to grab hold of him.

His kiss was hot and greedy, his hands roamed fast and loose, and she gave herself up to the moment.

He pulled her as close as he could, pushing her shirt up enough to get to the smooth warm flesh beneath it. The world pitched out of its orbit. Yearning became gravity, the last reality, the only thing left to keep them earthbound.

Mutual need had their lips parting, and they gasped for air. She struggled with a cry of desperation in her throat, and he kissed her there as he palmed her breast, his fingers telling of his urgency.

"Mich," he murmured close to her ear. Waves of pleasure rippled through her, and she gave in to it, floated senseless and weak in its current.

He felt her surrender and pulled away to look at her, her eyes glazed with rapture and need, her lips wet and ready for him.

"Michelin," he said to get her attention, needing to know if he could have her now or if any part of her was still angry with him enough to make her regret it later. "Now is the time to tell me to stop . . . if you want me to." The strain in his voice was clear.

"No," she breathed, pulling his face back to hers, kissing him wantonly.

All systems were go, yet even as he closed his eyes Noah saw a blue light strobing across the back of his mind. Close enough, he thought, his fingers racing to the hooks on her bra, his hands aching for the weight of her breasts.

"Noah," she muttered, ripping the snaps on the front of his shirt open.

"Snaps. I'll never underestimate a cowboy's sartorial taste again," he said, his mouth busy at her neck as he fumbled with the buttons on her shirt.

She giggled, and at the same time he flipped her blouse open. So beautiful. He took one rosy-tipped nipple into his mouth, drew his tongue across the tip, then suckled. Her happiness mingled with pleasure was a sound unlike any he'd heard before. Sweeter than the morning larks of East Africa. More exotic than the village music of Burma. As mysterious as any night noise anywhere.

She yelped, and they both scrambled, all arms and legs, as they heard a loud thump on the truck door behind them.

Over her shoulder, Noah saw the classic trooper hat and dark glasses of the Highway Patrol and immediately checked to make sure they'd gotten completely off the road.

"Any trouble here?" the man asked in a deep, trained-to-be-frightening voice. The window was open, and his hand was on the door. "On second thought, if you're heading for Vegas, these little roadside stops are like putting the cart before the horse, don't you think?"

They both sputtered and spoke quickly, denying everything from even owning a cart to heading to Las Vegas.

"Well, now that you've pulled yourselves together, would you mind stepping out of the vehicle?" He asked his question, then stepped away to examine the camper, a rusty affair that was set snug in the flatbed of an ordinary pickup truck—which had also seen better days.

The heat in their faces gradually cooled in the midmorning sun, and their heart rates returned to normal as the officer explained that he'd stopped due to his concern about the safety of the vehicle. Michelin had only to assure him that it was legally functional, show ownership, pass an impromptu safety examination, and he drove off with a wave and an amused grin.

For the first time since they were interrupted, their gazes met and held. Memories flooded back. The delight. The abandon. The fear. The embarrassment.

They leaned against the back of the camper and burst into laughter.

"I felt like a little kid," she said, wiping a tear from her eye.

"Caught in the backseat of our parents' car at Lovers' Leap," he added, chuckling.

They laughed a little longer, began to feel hot again, and decided to get cold drinks from inside the camper.

"It's just a darn good thing he stopped when he did," she said, handing him his drink, slamming the camper door, and checking to make sure it was locked. "There's no telling what might have happened if he hadn't."

There wasn't?

He turned in a circle, watching her as she walked around him to the front of the truck. He frowned, then followed.

"What's that supposed to mean?"

"We could have ruined our friendship," she said, serious as organ music. "Nothing can kill a friendship faster than sex. You know that."

"No, I don't."

"Of course you do."

"No. I don't."

"Then trust me," she said, opening the door of the cab and climbing in. "A sexual relationship is the last thing we need right now."

"How are you figuring this? Judging by what just happened—"

"Exactly." She nodded emphatically. "See. You know as well as I do that once we start having sex, we'll never stop. The attraction or chemistry or magic or whatever it is between us is so powerful, we'd be tearing each other's clothes off every chance we got. We wouldn't be able to think of anything else."

"So?" He saw no problem.

"So, the sex would taint the results of our experiment. How would we know if we were really truly friends or just afraid of losing a great sex partner? Don't we tolerate certain things in a lover that we wouldn't tolerate in a friend, and vice versa? Friends have a true clear picture of each other and they're free to walk away at any time. But with lovers, there's always the sex. Clouding the issues. Influencing decisions. It becomes like a weapon they can use against each other. A weapon real friends don't need or want."

She seemed very decisive on this matter, sounded a little like Dr. Joyce Brothers. Still he had to ask, "You're sure about this?"

"Absolutely," she said, closing the door. She was about to start up the engine, then changed her mind. "You could probably tell I enjoyed what we did."

He nodded. "That was the impression I got."

"Well, generally speaking, I do like sex. A lot. And I'm easily tempted, so you're going to have to help me."

"Help you?" He was beginning not to like this conversation.

"As my friend it's your responsibility to help me resist any urges I might have to make love to you," she said sincerely, her expression guileless and earnest.

"You're kidding, right?"

She looked away briefly, then back at him with sympathy and understanding.

"I know. It isn't fair of me to ask you this favor, but

I want, so much, for us to be friends. And I'm afraid that if we have sex before we're both ready . . ." Her chin quivered slightly; she pressed her lips together and looked away.

"Okay," he said quickly, feeling like a traitor to his own sex, thinking a man who was less honest and forthright, who was less cautious and less concerned with the quickest best solution to a problem, would undoubtedly be able to come up with a more satisfactory arrangement. But, as it was . . .

"We'll do it your way. We'll wait and . . . and I'll do my best to help you curb your urges," he said, shaking his head. He left her window to walk around the front of the truck and get in. "What have I done?" he muttered under his breath, sweeping his dark hair with his fingers, missing the wily smirk that skipped across her lips.

NINE

"What have I done?" He pondered the question once again, as he had the previous evening. They'd taken separate rooms at the Holiday Inn, and he had to use his key card twice to get the door open. "Where'd I go wrong?"

He dropped his duffel on the floor, threw the card on the dresser, and fell backward onto the bed, spread-eagle.

"What happened?" he asked himself, recalling the strange moment that occurred between the time he was filled with hope and hungry passion and his realization that there was no silver lining to this cloud. A good arbitrator always knew the instant his case took a turn for the worse. The moment he agreed to her terms, he knew he was in trouble. And he'd been in and out of hot water so often since then, he was beginning to feel like a tea bag.

They'd driven the better part of the day away, art-fully dodging topics connected to their relationship, fo-

cusing instead on subjects ranging from the ridiculous
—his first visit to a pygmy hut and the subsequent roof
raising that followed—to the sublime—how small and
yet incredibly unique she'd felt the summer she took
Eric to see the Grand Canyon.

The sun was beginning to set, casting a fire-red hue
across the desert and mountains, making them look as if
they were smoldering hot, sizzling, when Mich finally
turned off onto an unmarked road.

"Eric and I have camped on this road before. We
use the mile signs to identify it—his idea. Sometimes
he's so smart and clever, it scares me."

"But most of the time it reassures you."

"Yes," she said, glancing at him, smiling at his per-
ceptiveness. "Most of the time it reassures me. I don't
think he's going to spend his whole life in a small town
full of people he knows and trusts. I don't even want
him to. I want him to see and do everything. But he's so
open and honest and trusting, I'm afraid he'll be hurt
when he discovers what the rest of the world is like."

So far, Noah had witnessed Eric's anger, his will to
fight and protect what was his, seen him deviously stuff
oil rags up the tailpipe of a car and lie by withholding
the truth—but he knew what she meant.

"He'll be hurt and he won't be innocent anymore,
but he's a tough kid—molded well by loving hands.
When I first met him, I worried about the home teaching and the small town and the people he associated
with, but . . ." He shook his head. How could he tell
her he envied the boy? "If all kids were as lucky . . . if
they were all as sure of themselves and knew so many
people cared about them . . ." Once again he shook

his head, contemplating the possibilities of world peace and harmony.

She, on the other hand, was contemplating him.

"What?" he asked, when he caught her looking his way, an uneasiness squirming in his belly.

"Did you think of taking him away from me when you first met him?"

This is a test. The National Security Alarm was buzzing in his head.

"Yes," he admitted. "For half a second. And then the plan was to take you both away because I knew he'd never leave you willingly."

She nodded and seemed satisfied. "And now you've changed your mind."

"Now it's up to you and Eric. To leave or stay in Gypsum. I can live anywhere, as long as you're there,'" he added, waiting for her to look at him, to see the truth in his face.

She did and she could, and she trembled from the magnitude of it. Her little scheme to teach him a lesson and drive him crazy at the same time wasn't going to work. He wasn't the volatile, masterful, sweep-her-off-her-feet-and-carry-her-away sort of hero she dreamed of as a girl. He was the steady, faithful, stand-beside-her-and-never-leave-her-no-matter-what sort of hero she needed as a woman.

Still, it was always good to know your limits, she thought, frowning and pointing a finger at him.

"Watch it. That sort of talk can be dangerous. There's always a certain . . . possessiveness in a friendship, but you have to be very careful not to let it get out of control. Oh! There, see there? That's our pit."

Baffled, he was mentally looking up the definition of possessiveness and scanning the flat desert terrain for rocks at the same time. He found the rocks first, when she pulled off the dirt road and stopped beside them.

She rolled the stiffness around in her shoulders and neck, grimacing. "Maybe I should have let you drive after all. My muscles are all bunched up and tight." She slid out from behind the steering wheel, turning her back to him. "Feel this. Just feel it. They're like rocks."

His hesitation to touch her made her smile. Then her lips drooped, her face sagged, and her muscles went nearly limp in the ecstasy that followed the path of his fingers and hands across the top of her back.

The whimper of pain/pleasure that escaped her started a slow cerebral meltdown. He had his hands close enough to her neck that to curl his fingers around it and squeeze hard was tempting, especially given the games she was playing. She started to purr, and he thought of the time they were wasting, time in which they could be hot and loving in each other's arms. Her body grew weak and pliant in his hands, and he felt an inkling of resentment—sure, she had a certain right to make him pay for his lie, but how expensive could one little deception be?

"Mmmm . . . I think you and I were destined to be friends," she mumbled, her chin on her chest. "I have the knots and you have the magic fingers."

Putting a knot on her head was beginning to appeal to him. A thin layer of sweat beaded on his forehead as he stewed in his own hormones. He shifted his weight uneasily, found no comfort, and guessed he wouldn't find any till he gave her what she wanted.

"I could work a lot more magic than this, if you want to lie down flat," he said, his tone deliberately suggestive.

"Mmmm . . . what?"

"Spread a blanket out under the stars. Loosen your clothes. Get comfortable."

She groaned.

He eased her back against his chest, his hands moving down her arms. "We'll start a fire to keep the chill away. . . ."

"Ah, you know, I feel better already," she said, straightening and scooting away. "That was great. Thanks. Really, I'm loose as a noodle. I think you missed your true calling . . . shoulda been a masseur."

He smiled and chuckled half a laugh at her speedy getaway. The only thing saving her from him was that he knew she was suffering as much as he was. Her pride and stubbornness were all that were keeping them apart —poor companions when your heart was full of love and your body was throbbing with lust.

They worked together unloading the camper, Mich the sleeping gear and food, Noah the kindling and wood for the fire that was bouncing and bright before the sun completely disappeared. They shared the cold supper from the Saloon and lingered over coffee, made thick and strong over the campfire.

"You're kidding," she said, laughing when he told her he'd yet to speak to Greta. "You've been there almost a week."

"I know. And I have yet to speak one word to her.

She's either gone somewhere or passed out cold on the couch. I make the bed, she tears it apart, changes the sheets, leaves fresh towels, and I never see her. Just little signs that she's been there. There's coffee and a cold breakfast every morning, but no Greta. In the afternoon there are cookies and more coffee and Greta passed out on the couch, neat as a pin." He shook his head.

"That's weird. She'll talk your ear off if you let her, and with you being so polite and courteous . . . On second thought, maybe you shouldn't be complaining." She tossed the coffee grounds from the bottom of her tin cup and stood up to stretch.

"Why do you say that?"

"What?"

"That I'm *so* polite and courteous."

"Because you are," she said, climbing into her sleeping bag, fully dressed except for her shoes. Noah's eyes covered the territory from her bag on one side of the fire to his on the other side, and bit down hard on the exasperation that welled up inside him. "And you don't have to get defensive about it. I like the way you are." She grunted a bit as she squirmed about in her bag. "I didn't know brothers could be so completely and totally different. In fact," she said, huffing as she pulled her jeans out from under her, folded them neatly in half, rolled them from hem to waist, then settled them under her head like a pillow. She rolled to her side to face him. "I think that's why I didn't recognize you at first. I mean, the physical resemblance is so obvious. But who you are, the way you are inside is so different it . . . well, it even changes the way you look on the outside."

"We were different people," he said with a shrug.

"We saw things differently. I suppose you could say we adapted to our environment differently."

"You did. Eric never adapted to anything. He was stuck at age two, demanding attention, pitching fits to get his own way, testing all the boundaries. You found peace somewhere. Eric never did." She hesitated. "I think sometimes . . . he wanted to die."

He looked at her steadily, not voicing the questions in his eyes that weren't even questions really as much as suspicions needing confirmation.

"I only rode on that motorcycle twice with him. The second time I told him he could kill himself if he wanted to, but I wasn't going with him. Even after we found out about the baby, it didn't change that look in his eyes. He was excited about it, made all sorts of plans, but"—she frowned—"it wasn't enough to fill the emptiness in him. Wasn't enough to make him cautious. Wasn't enough to make him want to live."

His gaze gravitated back to the fire, but he couldn't see the dancing flames, the light didn't penetrate the smoky procession of the memories inside his head. Recollections of the fear that had grabbed at him when the phone rang late at night, when police cars pulled up to the front porch, or ambulances squealed through the streets. Echoes of his own voice asking his brother if he was trying to kill himself, wondering aloud about his mental stability, and furiously demanding explanations for the unexplainable.

"You," she said in a soft voice. "You learned to survive. You must have felt just as unwanted, just as lonely. But maybe the child in you remembered what it was to be loved. Maybe you knew things could be different, and you were smart enough to look somewhere else, other than to your father, for the approval and encouragement you needed. I don't know." She paused and was thoughtful, looking at him. "There's an unshakableness about you. A quiet determination, I guess. You remind me of the sort of person who, if you wanted to go to China, wouldn't whine about the fact that you couldn't walk there or steal because you couldn't afford the airfare or give up and become disheartened because you couldn't have what you wanted. You'd start digging a hole," she said, and when his eyes left the fire to meet hers, she went on. "And you'd dig and dig and dig and dig until you finally came out on the other side of the world, in China."

They stared at each other for a good long minute, then Noah started to laugh.

"I would never dig a hole to China. The engineering alone involved in a project like that would boggle my mind." Still, he knew what she meant. "I'd probably take a minimum-wage job as a . . . a . . ."

"As a tomato picker," she offered helpfully, smiling.

"As a tomato picker. Save every penny I made for the next twenty years, and *then* I'd buy a ticket to China."

"Okay. But you'd get there. Eventually. Right?"

"Right." He smiled at her, his heart warmed by the idea that she'd given his nature so much consideration, that she'd come to the conclusion that he was not altogether loathsome or despicable, but someone almost admirable.

"Right," she repeated, hesitating to go on. "Well, what I was getting at was that if you still feel guilty about leaving Eric when you did, you shouldn't. I think, maybe, it was part of your instinctive plan to survive." She looked away briefly, then back. "Like maybe you knew somehow that he was a sinking ship—that he'd waste your life, too, if you let him."

If he'd had those thoughts himself fifteen years before, they weren't conscious.

It rubbed against every fiber of his being to think he'd abandon a loved one in need—but was self-preservation such a horrible thing?

He shook his head and murmured his regret. "I shouldn't have left him."

"No. Then that would mean I should have gone with him that day. He asked me to. He was bored. He wanted to go raise some hell in Vegas. I did, too, but he wouldn't go with me in the truck, and I wouldn't ride with him on the Harley. We fought, and I told him to go without me." She waited for him to look at her. "Does that mean I should have gone with him, that I should have died with him? Or was that some subconscious force that recognized his self-destructiveness and kept me and my child alive?"

"But you said the other day that I abandoned him."

"I was wrong. I didn't know then what I know now. I didn't know you. But I've had a long time to deal with my own guilt about that day. And every time I look at my son, I know I made the right decision. Just like I know you did."

Receiving her absolution was like a balm to his tortured soul. He couldn't think of anything to say, but stared into the fire as he fit puzzle pieces together in his head. By the time he had enough of the pieces joined so that a clearer picture of his life was beginning to emerge, she'd rolled away from him and the fire and gone to sleep.

He crawled into his own sleeping bag with a contented sigh. He'd traveled the world enough, seen enough, experienced enough to know that there were forces in the universe beyond any man's control. So maybe he had been a bit arrogant in thinking he might have altered the outcome of his brother's life. Maybe everything in his life was just as it was meant to be. And maybe, just maybe, it was time to let Eric rest in peace.

By morning, the true degree of control he had over his life was perfectly clear. He had none. He was in over his head.

"Do you always drive this slow?" she asked, the peevishness she woke up with sharpening the edges of her voice.

"I'm ten over the limit."

"Are you sure? It feels like we're crawling."

"We're not crawling. If we go any faster, this rusty old bucket will fall apart."

"There's not a thing wrong with this vehicle. I checked it out myself."

"It's all over the road," he said. "It's a good thing that cop didn't see this thing in motion yesterday. By the way, the gas gauge hasn't moved in an hour."

"It's broken, but if you'd just keep the speed steady and stop slowing down, we'll have plenty of gas."

"I'm ten over the limit."

She leaned over to check the speedometer.

"Are you *sure* you don't want to drive?" he asked.

"No. I'm nervous enough as it is. I just wish you'd drive a little faster. I don't want to be late."

"We're not going to be late. We're an hour from Flagstaff, and the weigh-ins don't start for another four hours. We have plenty of time."

"Not if we're crawling," she muttered. When he glared over at her she was placidly looking out the window.

He took a firmer grip on the wheel and a deep, bracing breath to calm himself. If this was another one of her friendship tests, it was a doozy. It had taken her less than ten minutes to wake up, pack up, and get back on the road at the crack of dawn. They'd stopped to wash up and eat breakfast in a small town that had reminded him a lot of Gypsum in its nowhereness, and she'd rushed him through that too. He'd taken his second cup of coffee to go.

He was aware that friends were, on occasion, expected to tolerate a pal's distempered mood swings and pretournament jitters, but he couldn't shake the feeling that more than a little hostility was mixed in with her purple funk, and that she was directing it at him.

"Once we get to the motel, there'll be time for a nice hot shower and a nap, too, maybe," he said, taking another stab at helpful encouragement.

"A nap? What for? I'm not tired, I'm nervous." She turned her head to look out the window again. "I have a lot riding on this, you know." She looked back at him. "And don't start in on all that money sitting in the bank, waiting to be used. I've been planning this for years. The timing. The money. Eric's school. I have to go through with it. It would be like . . . like planning a party and then not having it, because someone else's party sounded like more fun and less work."

"It was just a suggestion, the nap. And I wouldn't dream of trying to talk you out of competing. I can't wait."

"You think it's dumb."

"Arm wrestling? No, I don't. Well, at first I thought of it as a kids' game, but not now. Not since Otis showed me the videos of last year's tournament in New York. I'm just surprised more people don't know about it."

"Well, you can't tell me you think it's a very feminine sport."

"A what?"

"Something a woman should be doing. You probably think women who arm-wrestle are mannish."

"No," he said slowly, choosing his words wisely. "I don't think *what* a woman does determines her femininity as much as *how* she does it. I've seen women here and in other countries working right alongside the men, soldiering with them, killing and dying with them. That doesn't make them less of a woman." Their gazes met briefly. "A woman's femininity comes from inside, like her charm and her compassion and her courage." A deliberate pause. "Like yours does."

That seemed to be enough for her to chew on as they passed through cattle country on their way into the pine forests surrounding Flagstaff.

"Is it the extra traffic or have you been driving this close to the center line all along?" she asked, leaning over to make sure he wasn't in the wrong lane altogether. "It's a little nerve-racking, don't you think, with those other cars—"

"Michelin?" he broke in calmly.

"What?"

"You're a really rotten passenger." She gaped at him. "Always have to be in control, don't you?"

"No. It's just that you're so close—"

"No. It's just that you're not used to looking out the windshield from that side of a truck. You're always in the driver's seat. Always had to be. But not anymore. If we're going to be *friends*," he said, turning her terminology back on her. "You're going to have to learn to trust me. I've been driving longer than you have. I have an excellent driving record. I *know* how to drive."

"I know, but the oncoming cars—"

"No buts. You either trust me to drive this thing or you don't."

"Fine. Drive the center line," she said, wiggling back securely into the seat. "I won't say another word."

He laughed. Not as much at her behavior as at his surprise at her acquiescence. Given the ultimatum, he'd fully expected her to demand the wheel back.

Instead, she smoothly navigated the route to the motel for him, giving him plenty of notice of direction changes, cringing once—silently—during a right turn she thought he'd taken too wide.

That she was still tense was clear in her silence and dogged adherence to the routine of unpacking the camper and checking into their rooms. They both took a key card from the clerk, listened patiently to his instructions, and wandered down a glass-enclosed hall to find their rooms.

"Well, look at that," she exclaimed, glancing from the number on the door to the camper parked outside. "We guessed pretty good, huh? We won't have to move the camper."

"Nope," he said, stopping beside the door just past hers.

"And we're right next door to each other."

"Yep."

He looked at her and couldn't decide if he wanted to strangle her or hug her. They shared a moment of mutual, silent regret that the rooms weren't connecting. Then she stubbornly slipped her card in the lock and went inside.

"What have I done?" She pondered the question once again, as she had most of the previous evening. "Where'd I go wrong?"

She dropped her suitcase on the floor, threw the card on the dresser, and fell backward onto the bed, spread-eagle.

She hadn't wanted him to agree to her terms. None of it was what she wanted. It was as if she were possessed by some . . . some . . . naughty nymph bent on stirring up trouble. What was she doing? Teasing him and taunting him, goading him like a mean little kid with a cattle prod, when all she *really* wanted was to be held in his arms again, to feel his lips against hers again, and to ease the ache of yearning that was tormenting her every moment, day and night.

How long had she watched him the night before, waiting to hear him settle in for the night, listening to him breathe, then turning over to memorize every curve and angle of his face, to count the steady pulse beats in his neck, to fantasize and dream without sleeping.

She covered her face with her arms and kicked her feet wildly in frustration, then rolled over on her side and curled into a ball.

She hated that everything was so easy for him. That's what it was. He walks into her life, and she falls like a ton of bricks for him. He drives her crazy for days with his standoffishness, and she throws herself at him. He confesses to lying, she understands why and forgives him almost immediately. Where was the fairness in this? Where was the fifty-fifty-ness?

No one valued anything that came to them too easily, that was human nature. Too often good fortune was taken for granted. Boasted about sometimes. Envied. Occasionally, people remembered to be grateful for it, but how often was it truly valued? Treated as something fragile? Cherished? Protected?

Not often, unless it was something hard-won, long-wanted, or rare.

That's what she wanted, she thought, drawing her arms tight against her chest, closing in on the deep, deep longing in her soul. With all her heart she wanted to be something rare, long-wanted, and hard-won. Cherished. Protected. Treated as something fragile.

Was that too much to ask?

It wasn't that loving Noah was difficult. Loving him was easy. Loving him felt like the most right thing she'd ever done. But she'd given her heart easily before, and it hadn't . . . really mattered. She'd given Eric her love and he'd given her what he had to give, but it hadn't been enough. Owning her heart wasn't enough to ease his pain, to fill his emptiness, to make him want to live . . . it wasn't something he'd treasured. It wasn't something anyone *treasured.*

That's what she wanted, to be the prize. Coveted. Costly. Conquered. Precious.

Just once.

TEN

Flagstaff, for all intents and purposes, was a tourist resort and a college town, home of the Northern Arizona Lumberjacks—owing their name, no doubt, to the town's primary exports of lumber, paper products, and construction materials.

And it offered a vast array of gathering places for a regional arm-wrestling competition.

"Eddy's?" Noah asked, amused, standing outside the designated site. "Eddy's? Think it's a good omen that it's being held in a tavern called Eddy's? I mean, what are the chances of this happening if it wasn't a good omen?"

"Beats me." She would have liked to laugh and been amused by it as well, but she simply wasn't. She was scared. Her chest was tight and her hands were clammy. She wanted to go home.

"Mich," he said, settling a comforting hand on her shoulder, bending his knees a bit to look into her downcast eyes. "It's an arm-wrestling contest, not another custody hearing. Relax. You can't lose anything here."

This was true—but only in the broadest possible sense. There was the money, of course, but there was also the family name and her face. Another good thought—she wasn't Japanese. Hara-kiri wouldn't be required if she made a complete fool of herself.

"Take a deep breath," he said, and she did. "Attagirl. Now hold your head up, walk in there, and intimidate the hell out of 'em. Tomorrow night you'll wipe the floor with them."

She couldn't help it, she laughed.

"Some peaceful ambassador you are." She reached out to straighten the collar on his black shirt. Clearly he'd gone back to the Bathhouse and picked out more clothes without her. Dressed completely in black, he was impressive, to say the least. Neon lights from within cast his features into mysterious and exciting shadows, like the tall handsome stranger in a Clint Eastwood movie. "Next I'll hear you yelling, 'Break the arm, killer.' "

"Ah, no. Not my style," he said, smiling back at her. "But I'll be thinking it."

She chuckled and looked away, fearing she might have tears in her eyes.

"I have a question," he said. And when she looked at him, he asked, "Are friends allowed to give hugs? You know, just in case one of them might need one?"

Without a second thought she moved into his arms and wrapped hers around him. She didn't know whom he was referring to, but *she* needed a hug. Bad.

A hot and cold chill swept through him. His eyes

closed, and he held her close. They sighed together and clung to each other for a good long minute, might have stayed that way all night if the bar door hadn't opened to let a small group of college students out.

"You ready . . . killer?"

"Yeah." She let loose a deep bracing breath. "I am ready."

He opened the door for her. "Let's hear your growl." She giggled and grrred. "Don't break any arms unless you absolutely can't help yourself, okay?"

She entered the dark hole with a smile on her face and a lightness in her heart that gave her an air of confidence, her long lithe body standing tall and graceful. Noah's heart almost burst with love and pride.

A great deal of socializing was involved with the official weigh-ins. Noah and Mich were there an hour, meeting people, greeting old friends and acquaintances from previous matches with a hug or handshake or a slap on the back.

When they finally made their way to the back of the room to the registration table and scales, the whole operation took less than five minutes. She signed the entry form and stepped on the scale.

"You look like you're feeling better," he said sometime later, setting two glasses and a pitcher of beer on the table in front of her, controlling his voice to be heard over the music and chatter.

"It's all an act," she said, pouring a glass for him, then herself. She'd had several beers already with friends and well-wishers, and was feeling much, much, much better. "There's some really great people here tonight, but tomorrow they'll be my opponents . . . and some of them are really good."

He smiled at her, unworried. When she simply sat there staring at him, he asked, "Are you all right?"

She nodded. "I'm just glad you're here."

"Yeah?"

"Yes. All you're expecting is something you've never seen before." She smiled down at her beer, then looked up. "Dad and my brothers—and Eric too—they're expecting me to win." She looked away.

"You're not thinking it would change the way they feel about you if you lost, are you?" he asked, knowing she was unaware of the power she had over the men in her life.

She lifted one shoulder and let it drop uncertainly. "They'd still love me, I guess. Let me keep my last name." She gave him a small smile. "But they're hard people to disappoint."

He had a flash picture of a dark-haired little girl running with all her might, working twice as hard, pretending to be tougher than she was to keep up with her older, stronger, faster brothers . . . thinking all along that to fail would be a greater disappointment to them than it was to her.

"I don't think there's anything in the world you could do that would disappoint your dad or your brothers, or even your son. They worship you." She laughed and opened her mouth to argue, but he held up his hand and stopped her. "I'm the outsider. I can see it, Mich. They respect you. They defer to your judgment. They trust your clear thinking. They admire your strength of will." He could see the doubt in her expression. "They focus on you, the home you make for them, the things you do for them, as their center of gravity." He glanced away, then back. "I know this, because I do too. I can see what I'm feeling in them. It's what the five of us identify with in one another, the only thing we have in common. It doesn't matter to any of us if you win or lose this contest. All any of us wants is for you to be happy." He paused when a fellow merrymaker bumped into the back of Mich's chair, and she had to right herself and refocus.

She raised her gaze to meet his, but he didn't have a chance to see what was in her eyes. "Well, excuse you," the man who'd bumped into her said. "This is a brand-new shirt, lady."

Both Noah and Mich turned to look at the man with half a glass of beer on his shirt and drunken anger on his face. He was tall and extremely ugly.

"Sorry," she said, feeling no remorse for what was, after all, his clumsiness.

"Sorry? This is a new shirt."

"Then you should watch where you're going," she said, having already apologized unnecessarily.

"Me? You're the one who bumped me."

"I don't think so. You're the one walking around with a beer in his hand. I was just sitting here."

"You bumped me. With your head."

"I didn't bump you. You stumbled over me."

"You bumped me."

"No, I didn't." She had never been very tolerant of mean, bossy drunks. "Why don't you go sit somewhere before you fall down . . . again."

"What about my shirt?"

"What about it?" she asked, her spirits rising to the occasion.

"It has beer on it."

"So now it's ugly *and* wet. What do you want me to do about it?"

Noah had very little experience with honky-tonk brawls—but he knew trouble when he saw it. "How about we buy you another drink and call it even?" he offered.

"How about you pay for the shirt and get a muzzle for her?"

"Oh now—"

"Me? A muzzle?" She stood up. "Look, pal, you may think you're some big cheese around here, but the fact is, you only smell like one."

"Mich . . ." Noah tried to quiet her with a grimace.

"Oh. Aren't you clever," the man said, his face bent low into Michelin's. "I'll bet your idea of an exciting night is turning on an electric blanket."

"Well, *I* bet you could sue your brain for nonsupport." She taunted the man without blinking, her hand closing around the handle on the pitcher of beer.

Noah, seeing this, put his hand on top of the pitcher to keep it from moving, and stood to make himself heard. "This isn't getting us anywhere," he said calmly. "How about you both apologize and go your separate ways."

"Apologize?" That caught her attention and had her frowning at him. "For what? I didn't do anything. *And* I've already said I was sorry he spilled beer on himself." She turned back to the man and said with great dignity,

"However, if I've said anything to insult you, you have to believe me, I've tried my best."

"Mich!"

"That does it, girly, somebody's got to shut that big mouth of yours."

"No! No," Noah said, holding his hand up to the man to stop him as he grabbed her arm and pulled her to his side. "That won't be necessary. This was just an unfortunate accident, and I'll be happy to pay to have the shirt cleaned. How's that? And the offer for the drink stands."

The man took half a second to think it over and was beginning to look satisfied . . . but not Mich.

"Are you nuts?" she asked. "He's lying. You can tell he's lying, his lips are moving."

"What is your problem, lady?"

"Mister, I don't like your face."

"Mich! For God's sake—" Noah pushed her behind him as the man took a step forward. "No. She's . . . she's not herself tonight. She's, ah, in the competition tomorrow and she's nervous, is all. She doesn't know what she's saying."

"The hell I don't."

He turned his back on the man, covered Mich's mouth with his hand, then spoke over his shoulder. "We're leaving. Here's ten bucks to clean the shirt. Help yourself to the beer there. Good night."

He started push-walking her to the front door.

"You oughta rethink that muzzle, buddy," the man called, filling his glass from the pitcher that had been mere seconds away from smashing in the side of his head.

Mich was hissing and sputtering and mad as a wet cat by the time he released her in the parking lot.

"*What* are you doing?" she asked with her first good breath. "That guy was a jerk. I was gonna push his face in."

"And that would have proved what? Accomplished what?"

"It would have proved he was wrong and a blowhard and a wuss. And it would have made me feel great."

"No one feels great after a fight."

"How would you know? I bet you never fight," she said. She wasn't sure where the words had come from, but they surely did make sense to her.

He wasn't a fighter. He wouldn't stop people from eating off his plate, refuse to wear funny-looking clothes someone else picked out for him, bicker about *anything*. She'd taunted him, attacked him, and teased him, and yet his temper seemed never to come close to boiling.

"What good does fighting do anyone?" he asked, walking toward the camper, still a bit incredulous at her behavior.

"It gets you what you want."

"Not always. Usually two people fight, hurt each other, and walk away empty-handed. There are other ways to get what you want, other ways to settle disputes."

"Talking?" she asked, her voice thick with sarcasm.

"Talking, waiting, bargaining, compromising, flipping a coin, trickery, judicial intervention—"

"You mean, you don't think anything is worth fighting for?"

"I don't think a beer-stained shirt is worth fighting for, no."

"What about principles?" she asked, refusing to climb into the truck as he held the door open for her. "What about insults?"

"What about them? What would the world be like if everyone felt free to punch out anyone who didn't have the same standards of morality they had? Or to beat up anyone who disagreed with them? And as for insults, haven't you ever heard about sticks and stones?"

"What *would* you fight for?"

Narrowing his eyes as if he were thinking real hard, he looked away and then back again. "Good question. Get in. I need to think on that one."

She got in but only because she was stunned stupid. Was that all part of his training? Peace at any cost? Was there nothing he thought worth fighting for? His country? His beliefs? Her?

No wonder she hadn't been able to get his goat—he didn't own one. She dreamed of being valued and treasured? How would she ever know it if he planned simply to outwait her? Or bargain for her love? Or trick her somehow? No. If it wasn't his country or his beliefs he'd fight for, then she wanted it to be her.

He got in and settled himself behind the steering wheel. She sat next to him, her arms folded across her chest, a mutinous pout on her lips. He made no attempt to start the engine but sat in the silence with her for a moment before he spoke.

"There *is* something I'd fight for," he announced quietly.

Well, shoot. What? The League of Nations? World peace? The abolition of tyranny?

"I'd fight for you. And for Eric. If I had to."

"If you *had* to?"

"If you were in immediate danger." It was a strange sensation to feel this absolute truth and to know in his heart that he was capable of delivering the punch he so abhorred. Man's inhumanity to man was a concept he'd understood early in his life.

"Define immediate danger," she said.

He turned the ignition and pulled out of the parking lot, analyzing this new insight into his character. When he spoke, he gave her the most honest answer he could.

"If every other means of extrication was exhausted, or if there was no time to try something else to remove you from harm, I'd resort to a punch."

She laughed. "Well, that was an uptown answer. You read that in a book somewhere?"

On the heels of this newfound capacity for violence, he also discovered a sudden shortness of temper.

"You're drunk."

"Not so drunk I don't know a spoiled little rich kid who's never had to fight for anything in his life when I see one. A man who hides behind diplomacy because it's easier and safer to talk the talk than to walk the walk."

"And stressed out about tomorrow," he said, making excuses for her as his knuckles turned white on the steering wheel.

"Maybe. But at least I know where to draw the line."

"What line?"

"*The* line. The one in the dirt. The one between you

and me. Whichever one of us has the guts to cross the line first gets to take the first swing."

"What the hell are you talking about?" he asked, finally pulling into a parking space in the motel lot, putting the truck in park, and turning to face her.

"I'm talking about *us*," she said, deciding not to finish the conversation in the truck. She opened the door and slid out. "I want things between us settled, once and for all, and now is as good a time as any."

He stared at the door she slammed in his face for a whole sixty seconds before reaching out to the door handle on his side. Odd, the mere admission of an ability to commit violence seemed to trigger it as a first response to a difficult situation. Either that, or she'd finally managed to drive him insane. He was ready to strangle her.

"Hold it right there," he said sternly as she opened the glass door to the hall on which their rooms were located. "*Don't* take another step."

She turned in the open doorway with a short laugh. "Or you'll what? Talk to me? Gimme a break," she said, the door closing behind her as she stepped inside.

She was inserting the key card into the lock when he came up behind her.

"I hope you have aspirin, and I recommend you take some tonight, because first thing tomorrow morning, you and I are going to have a long serious talk about all this."

The door opened. "Ahhh . . . nope. I don't think so," she said.

"You don't think so what? That you have any aspirin or that we're going to have a discussion?"

She turned to lean against the doorjamb. "Both, actually."

"Well, then you better think again, sweetheart, because you and I are—"

"Noah," she said in a voice he knew from his dreams. She looked up with eyes that were warm and tender, her lips soft and inviting. In spirit, he went to his knees. "I don't have to think anymore. I love you."

She was just now figuring this out? Had this been her problem all along? Was the crisis over at last? He saw *kiss me* in her expression and didn't waste another second to comply.

Pressing her tight against the doorjamb, he covered her mouth with his. She kissed him back and wrapped her arms about his neck. He inhaled her life's breath, filled his mind with the scent of her, his arms with the feel of her. She gave all she was to this kiss that meant life or death to her soul. He'd never known anything like it, felt the world in his hands, the future safe and happy in his hands.

With their world narrowed down to the space they occupied and their all-too-mortal lungs screaming for air, they held each other and sent prayers of gratitude and supplication heavenward.

"Mich," he murmured near her ear, and she closed her eyes as warm satisfaction flowed through her. "I love you."

"I know," she said, breathless, her heart aching as she eased away from him. "And I love you." Then, rolling back into her room, she added, "But if you want me, you're going to have to fight for me."

It was several more seconds before he realized he

was gaping at a closed door. The number "136" made him stop to think, but it didn't make any sense either. What had just happened? He replayed the scene in his mind, repeating her final words over and over as if they were in a foreign language.

How could he argue with someone he didn't understand? Women. Hadn't he just said he'd give his life for her? Wasn't that enough? His body was throbbing with need. He could still smell her scent in the air. At that moment he would have gladly bashed in any head she asked him to . . . although hers was the most tempting.

A horrible thought. A repulsive thought. She was driving him crazy, that's what she was doing. He was a man dangling by a thread at the end of his rope.

Mich listened to his steps in the hall, heard his door close, and then let loose the air that was stuck in her chest. *Was she possessed?* She covered her face with her hands, pushed her hair back, and held it at the nape of her neck. The alcohol in her blood had burned itself off, and she was thinking too clearly now. Remembering too well. She had to be possessed, it was the only explanation she had for her behavior.

Why couldn't she simply accept the fact that he loved her? That she loved him. She wasn't some princess in a glass tower, a maiden with long golden hair held captive by a witch. She wasn't a little girl who believed in fairy tales. She wasn't a woman waiting to be rescued by some knight on a white horse.

Or was she?

No, she decided, she wasn't any of those things. Truly. She was a simple woman who wanted to know the man she loved would go the extra mile for her. Would never take her love for granted. Would love her no matter what. And wasn't afraid—or too civilized—to show it to the world, shout it from the rooftops, carve it in a tree trunk.

Romance. The word made her roll her eyes with chagrin. The last thing she thought she wanted was some man fawning over her. But if she cared to be perfectly honest with herself, that's exactly what she did want. Just a little romance, enough to know she mattered to him—a lot.

There was nothing wrong with a calm coming together of two hearts and minds. Nothing unwelcome about a solid, uncomplicated love affair.

It was enough. It had to be. It was childish and foolish to wish for grand gestures that weren't necessary. Wasn't it?

Limp with relief, she sat down on the bed. She was glad she'd come to this decision; she'd learn to accept it and feel *so* much better. She sighed, thought about going next door to apologize and explain—then decided against it. She'd tell him first thing in the morning.

No more silly friendship-only business. No more taunting or teasing. Love would take its course without any more interference from her. No more lies. No more walls. No more extraordinary expectations.

She was asleep before her head hit the pillow that night. Content. At peace at last.

ELEVEN

The warm wet kiss he got when he opened the door was as unexpected as the bright smile on her face and the dazzling light in her eyes. "Good morning," she stepped back and said. "Please say you can forgive me. Call it cold feet, PMS, temporary insanity . . . whatever, I don't know, I can't think of a good enough excuse for the way I've been behaving. But I'm over it now, and if you'll just please forgive me, we can get on with our lives. Ready for breakfast?"

He stared a few seconds longer, cautious and curious, then turned back into his room to get his key and hat.

"No hangover?" he asked, starting for the exit.

"Nope. And I'm only half apologizing for that, drinking too much, because I think it was good for me. You know, like a vent. I got a lot of stuff off my chest last night. Silly stuff. And once it was out there, I could see how silly it was and . . . I'm over it. I feel great."

"You look great . . . like you feel great," he said, wary of his words. "You look like you feel great."

She laughed as she left the building. "Well good, because I do. And I just want you to know that other business is all over too."

"Which other business?"

"All of it. Everything." She buzzed his lips with hers, and because she was unaccustomed to making apologies, she changed the subject. "Eric and I have been here a couple of times to see the observatory. We can spend the day there if you want or walk over and check out the college or . . . I seem to remember some prehistoric ruins somewhere nearby."

"I think I'd rather go back to Eddy's."

"What? Now? What for?"

"That bigmouth last night looked like a regular, didn't he?" He didn't really wait for her to answer. "You were right about him. He needed to have his face pushed in. I feel like going back and doing it for him."

"What?"

"We can eat first if you want, but then I think we should go back. Wait all day for him if we have to."

"Noah. Stop. I said I was wrong. I made a fool of myself last night and—"

"No. No, you didn't. You were right. He bumped you. I saw him. And I should have made him apologize to you instead of paying to have his shirt cleaned. I'm just so used to smoothing things over, keeping everyone happy, taking the path of least resistance."

"But that's a good thing. Someone has to keep his head while the rest of the world goes insane." By some unspoken agreement, they were heading across the street to an Apple Barrel Family Restaurant. "I was a little drunk and a lot confused. If it weren't for you, the whole incident could have turned very ugly."

"The guy was a bully. You were right to stand up to him. One of the things I love best about you is that you don't let people walk all over you." Taking her arm, he led her into the street, or they'd have missed their chance to cross. "I never could do that," he said on the other side. "Stand up for myself. I learned other ways to get what I wanted, what I needed, but it was never the direct, physical approach. That was always too messy, too painful. And I . . . I was always too afraid of my father. It was easier to talk it out, charm it away, patiently outsmart the other guy. But I could do it, I think. Pound someone to a pulp." He smacked his left hand with his right fist. "I'm quick. I'm in shape. Not as in shape as I was when I worked the mines in Angola, but I know I can take that jerk from last night."

"Noah," she said, feeling worse than ever. "No. What I love about *you* is that you're not like that. I love that you're bright and clever and charming, that you're not violent. That you're kind and gentle and understanding. Please stop talking like this."

"I'm not just talkin'. I'm hot. I'm ready. I'm psyched."

"Well, get over it," she said, leading the way into the restaurant, missing the wily smirk that skipped across his lips. "It's done. He probably wouldn't remember what you were talking about, even if we did happen to see him again."

"Oh," he said sadly. "Well, it doesn't have to be him. Someone else is bound to tic me off eventually."

She turned, openmouthed, to stare at him. "You're kidding, right?"

"Do I look like I'm kidding?"

Well, no. He sure didn't. And to prove it, he glowered at a young man who happened to look up at them as they walked by his booth. "What you staring at?" he asked him.

"Noah!" She gave the young man a please-forgive-him-he's-mentally-handicapped look and pushed Noah toward the booth the hostess was holding for them. "What is the matter with you?"

"Nothing. That guy was starin' at you."

"Starin' at me? He's eighteen."

"Old enough to keep his eyes to himself."

She laughed. "Okay. I give up. You win. The joke's over."

"I'm starving," he said from behind his menu. "You can really work up an appetite when your adrenaline is flowing like this."

She read the cover of his menu, rubbing her lips together in indecision. Sometimes when Eric was "overtestosterized," it worked best simply to ignore his behavior until it ran its course. And since she had no better explanation or solution for Noah's present disposition, she remained silent and watchful.

Except for the fact that he glared narrowly at the busboy the whole time he was clearing the table next to them, their breakfast was pleasant and uneventful.

They drove up to Lowell Observatory, a university-related installation used primarily to discover and observe comets and discover and measure variable stars.

"Two years ago Eric and I took a field trip to Kitt

Peak National Observatory in Tucson, and that was amazing," she was telling him after the tour. They'd dallied a bit to enjoy the hilltop view of the land, and were now alone on the long concrete ramp leading down to the parking lot. "I spent the whole day there with my mouth open in wonder. It was incredible, beyond my imagination. I—"

Her last word was abruptly cut off as his mouth covered hers and his arms cut off her oxygen supply. A moment of surprise was short-lived, then she gave herself up to the hungry passions that were ever ready to consume her.

Staggering back together, they came to rest against the railing, pressed close, oblivious, weak with need.

"What are you doing?" she asked when she could, breathless, laughing, half-hysterical. "What are we doing here?"

"Taking a direct, physical approach," he said, his lips wet and tender on hers. "Very messy. Very painful. And I *like* it."

She giggled and squirmed as he tickled her neck with his mouth. "Well, maybe it does have its place . . . umm."

Her chatter was a distraction—nothing for him to do but start all over again. . . .

On tiptoe she stretched herself against him; he pressed her pelvis close and tight against his. He gathered fistfuls of the sweater she was wearing to keep from crushing her in his arms; she whimpered with desire.

"Aha," he said suddenly. She turned her head to look over the railing, where he'd spotted a small group of people on the level below.

"There's that guy from the tour. See him? In the red jacket? Stay here, I'm going to have a few words with him."

"What? Noah, stop. Why? What are you doing?"

"He and I are going to have it out right here. This won't take long, he looks like one of those science guys . . . a nerd."

"A nerd?" She wanted to laugh, but he looked completely serious. "You want to beat him up because he looks like a nerd?"

"No. I don't care if he's a nerd. He was lookin' at me funny in there during the tour."

"Lookin' at you funny?"

"Smiling at me."

"Smiling at you," she repeated, thinking quickly. "Well, that's stupid. My brothers wouldn't hit someone for smiling at them. They'd either smile back or ignore them."

"Yeah?"

"Oh yes. You really have to pick and choose wisely. If you're going to fight with someone, you have to have a darn good reason, or . . ."

"Or?"

"Or you're a bully. Like that guy last night."

He considered this for a moment, then looked at her. "Well, I don't want to be a bully. That was never the point."

"No, that would be even more out of character."

"I'm just not going to let people push me around anymore."

"Okay."

"Or be rude. I hate rude people."

"We all do," she said, humoring him.

She thought it was a stroke of genius to suggest the drive-through window at Burger King for a late lunch.

"No," he said slowly, addressing the speaker box through the window of the truck. "It's two Whoppers. Hold the onion and tomato on one. Hold just the onion on the other. Two fries. One large. One small. And two colas, both medium. If you want, I can come inside and tattoo it on your forehead."

Because it was in her own thinking pattern, she simply assumed their food had been spat upon and couldn't eat it . . . citing nerves for her lack of appetite—though she did find some comfort in watching him eat.

"You know what you are?" she asked, holding the glass door open behind her as he followed her into the hallway at the motel.

"A man among men? The best kisser you've ever known? The next popular candidate for president? The man of your dreams? The first man to—"

"You're an excellent distraction."

"That was my next guess," he said.

She laughed. "You are. I've hardly thought of the competition all day. If you hadn't been here, I'd have been a basket case by now, sitting around all day, worrying."

"And now you've only got two hours to sit around and worry and become a basket case. Well, I'm glad I could be of help."

She laughed again. "No. I'll be fine now. I'm going to take a shower, work out a little . . . what?"

He was shaking his head. "I haven't finished distracting you yet."

Her eyebrows rose and then slowly lowered on the nicest conclusion she could come to. A smile of appreciation and anticipation came to her lips. His was predatory. She was tingling all over as she slipped the card into the lock.

"Plan B sounds good too," she said, her heart pounding fast and erratic. Far away in some small dark corner of her heart lived a tiny hope that their first coming together would begin slightly more romantically than by his simple declaration that the time had come. But her hunger was so great, her need was clamoring so loud in her ears, her body was aching with such desire that it was easy to ignore such compunctions.

Inside her room, she tossed her purse on the dresser, then turned to him, eager, waiting, wanting him to attack her, to take her into his arms and ravage her. Her fingers were throbbing, longing to touch him.

"Take off your shirt and lie facedown on the bed," he ordered, disappearing into the bathroom.

The tiny hope in her heart screamed out in pain, and an excruciating sadness settled in her chest.

Noah saw it the moment he returned. His love for her, for the vulnerability so well hidden by the woman she'd become, soared to a new level—beyond anything he'd known before, beyond anything he could truly comprehend or define.

His smile was the most achingly tender thing she'd

ever known. He came to her, caressed her cheek with the back of his fingers, then lifted her face to his for the sweetest of all kisses.

Still tipping her chin toward him, he waited for her to open her eyes. "I love you more than anything or anyone I've ever known in my life," he said. "Do you believe that?"

She couldn't not believe it, it was too plain in his eyes. She nodded.

"Then I want you to know that the next time I come at you, I'm coming direct and physical. Head-on. And I'm taking everything. Your sharp little mind. Your huge heart. This gorgeous body. Everything. Does that scare you?"

She wasn't sure and she couldn't answer.

"That's okay," he said. "You should be scared. Because once it's done, there's no going back." He kissed her hard and quick. "Now take off your shirt and lie facedown on the bed."

Dazed and more than a little confused, she began to unbutton the front of her blouse. He turned his back on her to toe-heel his shoes off, rubbing something small and round between his palms.

She walked over to the bed and did what he'd asked, eyes growing wide when she felt his fingers unhook her bra and slide the straps off her shoulders.

"Lift up," he said, pulling the undergarment away when she did, then kneeling on the bed to straddle her hips. "Close your eyes," he said, closing his own and clenching his teeth against the intense pressure between his legs.

For a naturally honest, forthright, prudent, and

thrifty man, he was walking a very fine line. But the fact was, she'd crawled so far under his skin she was more a part of him than if they shared the same blood. She was so basic and so complicated . . . wanting someone steady and steadfast, dreaming of the danger and excitement of romance.

He poured the complementary lotion he'd taken from the bathroom into his palm and tried to ignore the thick lust that bubbled like hot tar through his veins as he smoothed it over the soft warm skin of her shoulders and back. Tears of frustration sprang to his eyes when she moaned with pleasure. He grimaced with the pain of his own need and wretchedly sought to take his thoughts elsewhere.

He supposed she was every woman, with her heart and her mind anchored close to the earth, but with some hidden secret part of her soul star-hopping in space—dreaming dreams, wishing wishes she often had to sacrifice for the greater, more practical part of herself, for the people she loved.

And he was every man, he supposed, who, even when deeply in love, was less fanciful, more direct, less intricate in his expectations and visions of the future. . . .

Kneading her tight muscles, he vowed, once again, that the woman beneath him would never again have to give up a dream or squelch a wish. If it took the rest of his life, every penny he had, every ounce of his energy and strength, every creative cell in his brain, he'd seek out and fulfill her every childhood daydream, her every silly wish, her every feminine hope. . . .

What did he know about love? What did he know

about women? Maybe it wasn't the sort of romance she wanted, but it was the best he could do. It was all he could think to give her in return for all she'd given him —for making sense of his life, for . . . making his life worth living. A few dreams come true. A few fantasies played out in real life.

So he'd stand by her side when she needed him to, and he'd take every opportunity that presented itself to make her life an exciting adventure. He smiled, anticipating the challenge of it.

So, okay. She'd been a little more tense than she thought, but if he thought he was helping her to relax, he was sadly mistaken. She might feel like a cooked noodle, but her mind was a whirling dervish. The small of her back would await the return of his magic fingers, and when they finally arrived to work those muscles, her brain would explode.

"Relax," he'd said, as if it were within her power. "Think about something else. I'm only human, you know. And if we're both thinking the same thing, we'll never make it to the competition."

She tried, but to no avail.

"Relax," he said again. He bent close to her upturned ear. "Okay. Picture two arms ready to wrestle. One's yours. The other one belongs to a female weight lifter on steroids, a hulking brute of a woman." She giggled. "Get the picture. *Just* that picture. Now picture the fight. The grip. The pressure. Then her arm goes. See it in your head."

Ungh, thwap. Huh, it worked. She tried it again. *Ungh, thwap.*

"Picture it over and over, until it becomes familiar."

Ungh, thwap. Ungh, thwap.

"Don't think about anything else. Just the two arms. The grip. The pressure. Then her arm goes."

Ungh, thwap. Ungh, thwap.

He said something else, but she was busy . . . *ungh, thwap. Ungh, thwap. Ungh* . . .

The phone in the room two doors down rang and rang. Then it rang in the room next door, and finally in her room. She waited for Noah to answer it, then realized he wasn't astride her anymore, wasn't massaging her back. He'd covered her with the spare blanket from the closet and left.

The phone kept ringing and she fumbled for it, rolling over on her back.

"Hi," he said over the line. "Have a nice nap?"

"Ummm. Why'd you leave?"

He chuckled. "I needed a cold shower."

Her smile was small, she wasn't sure if she should thank him or hang up on him. "Thanks for the massage. I needed one."

"I know, but don't thank me. I was under orders. Frankly, it was the hardest thing I've ever done."

"Under orders?"

"Your dad told me to either hire it done or do it myself, but to get you a good rubdown before you left for the tournament." He paused. "The thought of hiring someone to touch you almost drove me crazy. Doing it myself *did* drive me crazy. I was within seconds of attacking an unconscious woman."

Her smile grew.

"Now wipe that silly smirk off your face and get in the shower. It's almost time to leave."

"Wanna come scrub my back?"

"You're asking for it."

"Yes, I am."

He chuckled, and her chest filled with joy at the sound.

"Just take your shower, Michelin. You'll get yours."

"Promise?"

"Oh, yeah."

When she should have been a nervous wreck, she found herself grinning like the village idiot. She smacked her cheeks and tried to look sober and tough, but her face sprang right back to a grin and happiness lit her eyes.

She frowned at herself in the steamy bathroom mirror, tried to envision her opponents, but all she saw was a hairy, steroid-filled arm going down. *Ungh, thwap.*

They walked into Eddy's at five o'clock sharp, and she felt like the Queen of the Mountain, just because *he* was walking in behind her.

"Look at all these people," he said, shouting to be heard. "Are there always this many?"

She nodded, turning her head to yell back. "This is nothing. They rent convention halls for the national and world events. Those are three-day competitions."

"You're kidding." She shook her head as they were suddenly separated by a stream of people.

After a couple of minutes he caught sight of her again, bobbing along with the crowd, heading for the back of the building. Her arm shot up in the air and pointed in that direction, indicating she'd meet him back there somewhere.

Eddy's was big, more a dance club than a standard bar, with a kitchen and pool tables and arcade games—clearly a favorite gathering place for college students.

Noah noted that the press seemed to have their own slant on the proceedings, interviewing the tattooed biker types and grizzly-looking truckers and hardly noticing the tall slim minister and the bifocaled computer operators and wiry construction workers who made up the majority of the contestants.

It wasn't hard to pick out the players from the spectators either. Down to the last man—and woman—Noah could see the serious intent in their faces. It didn't matter to them that the sport officially got no respect, not to mention snooty snubs from the International Olympic Committee, for them it was a major sport, eons away from its barroom-brawl roots. As difficult as weight lifting, as basic as running, as competitive as any Olympic event on the roster.

By the time he reached the roped-off area in the back, the noise was deafening.

Three padded tables similar to the one at the Saloon in Gypsum were set up on the stage. On the dance floor below, the contestants sat in folding chairs, squeezing hand grips, stretching muscles. Others pumped iron till the very last second.

"Noah. Noah," he heard her shouting to him before he saw her to the far left of the roped-off area, relegated, it appeared, to the women's division. "I was beginning to think you'd changed your mind and gone home."

"No way. I wouldn't miss this for anything." He leaned forward to ask, "Are you sure these are all *female* women? That one over there looks like a Bulls linebacker."

"Different weight class, but she's actually won some bodybuilding competitions in California."

He nodded as he looked over the rest of the female competitors. Dividing them into three weight classes was easier then, and those in Mich's class didn't really look much different than she did. Some had more defined muscles, but some were smaller. Some had tattoos and were missing teeth; some looked as benign as kindergarten teachers.

"How do you feel?" he asked her.

She laughed. "I don't know. Scared. Excited. Stupid."

"Why stupid?"

"I'm gonna get creamed."

"No, you're not. Now picture it in your head. . . ." He turned her around by the shoulders and started kneading her muscles. "Look 'em straight in the eyes, growl a little if you can."

She turned back to him. "What I really need is a good-luck kiss to—"

Before she could finish, his mouth was on hers, hot, greedy, and full of pent-up passion. He filled her with a gnawing hunger, energized her, held her face between his hands until she looked at him.

"You are your own good luck, Mich. And you're already a winner in my eyes."

She smiled up at him as the announcer opened the competition with a hearty welcome to Eddy's.

While he introduced the officials in black-and-white-striped shirts and went over the rules sent to them by the AAA—the American Arm-wrestling Association, not the auto club—Noah started looking the crowd over with a finer eye for phase two of his plan.

She might have been a little tipsy when she told him he'd have to fight for her, might have even changed her mind when she sobered up, but the wish had come from somewhere. The seed of a dream to be wooed and won was planted somewhere in her heart, and he was going to make sure it bloomed for her—even if it killed him.

In the interest of saving time, three events were held at the same time, one at each table. Six at a time the contestants took to the stage amid thundering applause and encouraging shouts.

Michelin's first bout seemed to be a long time coming, though she was only tenth on the list. She cast him a quick glance when her name was called, then didn't look his way again as her mind locked down in concentration.

She faced a muscle builder from California, took less than the full one minute to grip—and lost.

It hurt like hell when she didn't return to his side and let him console her—until he realized her second pull was only two bouts after the first, and the trip through the chairs and other players would have been a waste of energy. He waited and waited for her to look his way, and when she finally could, he beamed a smile at her.

"See it," he shouted, pointing to his eyes because he knew she couldn't hear him. "In your head," he said, pointing there too.

Mich nodded that she understood, but it was going to take a heck of a lot more than just seeing it in her head to win this next pull and stay in the competition. All the people made her nervous, they weren't a saloon full of family and friends. The stakes were high—how could she go home if she lost in the first round? The money shrank in importance now that there were other options, but winning . . . oh, winning would show Noah that he was getting someone special and unique, she realized suddenly. Someone he could be proud of. Someone worth cherishing.

She glanced at him one more time when her name was announced. He grinned and shook his fist at her encouragingly, and she knew he'd be there to say all the right things if she lost again.

She stood across the table from a blonde aerobics instructor from Phoenix, who any other day of the year might be perky, bubbly, and friendly—but today she hadn't the slightest glimmer of amicability in her eyes.

Wordlessly they shook hands, then squared off at the table. Each took hold of the grip with her free hand and slipped her elbow into the talc-coated indentation in the padded table.

Focus. Focus. Mich repeated it in her head until the din of the cheering crowd was only an annoying buzz in her ears. She wrapped her fingers around the blonde's and had time for a really quick look at Noah—for good luck.

Once again he was pointing to his eyes and head. She took a deep bracing breath, and at the last instant decided what the heck. She conjured up the two arms in her mind, replaced the hairy one with the smooth slim arm of the aerobics instructor, and listened for the "Ready, go!"

Biceps bulged. Wrists wobbled and locked. Faces grimaced with pain and determination. Legs scrambled for balance. Mich could feel her arm leaning toward the table, backward, but that wasn't what she was seeing in her head.

In her head their arms were upright, and her opponent's began to slowly, slowly tip. In her head she saw them go down, hers on top. *Ungh, thwap!*

"Winner!"

The word echoed through her head like part of a dream, and it was several more seconds before she realized the referee was holding her hand in the air and the blonde was congratulating her.

"Yes! Yes! Thank you. Great pull. Thank you. Yes! I did it. Oh, God. Yes!"

She wasn't sure how she got off the stage and across the dance floor, but suddenly she was in Noah's arms.

"I did it. Did you see? I did it."

"Of course you did it," he said, lifting her off the floor and kissing her heartily. "That's my girl."

But that had been only the first elimination round, they soon realized, their high emotions swooping down to nervous anticipation again as if they were on a roller coaster.

TWELVE

Nearly a quarter of the contestants were eliminated in the first round. A floor official came by to inform them that Mich would pull twice again in the second round, in positions five and thirteen.

"My girlfriend goes second and tenth," a tall thin man with glasses commented, when the official walked away. "She's really nervous. 'Course, I don't know which of us is more nervous really, her or me."

When Noah simply looked down his nose at the man, Mich felt compelled to say, "I'll bet it's her. I'm pretty much a wreck myself."

He nodded and smiled. "She was throwing up all day today."

"Aww, that's too bad," she said, looking at Noah, knowing he'd feel bad for the woman too.

The man looked at Noah, too, assuming him to be a kindred spirit in this particular situation. But Noah was scowling at him.

"What are you doin'?" he asked the man belligerently. "Tryin' to psych her out?"

"What?"

"Listen, we don't need this. Take your sad stories and move on down the line, pal."

"I didn't mean . . ." the man sputtered.

"Yeah, right. It's the oldest trick in the book. Pick out a victim, strike up a conversation, bore them to tears with talk about nerves and throwing up and losing, plant seeds of doubt and weakness in their heads. Think we're stupid?"

"No. No, I . . ."

"Noah. I'm sure he—"

"Then get the hell away from us," Noah said, with every intention of apologizing to the poor guy later. "Go work on some other unsuspecting schmo."

The man, looking crushed and confused, attempted to say something, then shook his head and left.

"Are you out of your mind?" Mich asked, stunned by his behavior. "He wasn't trying to psych me out, he was just—"

"Mich," he said, grinning, leaning toward her. "I love this stuff. I've never intimidated anyone in my whole life. It makes me feel so . . . tough."

"Tough?"

"Yeah. Like I could take on the world—and win." He laughed. She thought it sounded a bit maniacal. "He was about my size, but he looked like a wimp, didn't he? I could have taken him easy, if he hadn't slithered away when he did. What a coward."

"Noah. You have to stop this. It's making me crazy.

How am I supposed to concentrate if I have to worry about you picking a fight with someone?"

"What? You think I'll get my face bashed in? I won't. I'm a lot stronger than I look, Mich. I don't work out in a gym, but look at my hands. I've worked in mines and on farms. Hard work. I know you think I'm a spoiled rich kid, but I haven't been one for years. I can't afford to be, not if I want to help. I've had to work alongside the working-class people of impoverished nations to know them, to know what they need most, to help them the best way I can. That's what I do, and it's made me strong. You don't have to worry about me. I can handle myself."

She stared at him openmouthed for a second or two. Who was this man? He knew as well as she did that fighting was useless and never proved anything. Still, he seemed so determined. As if he were bound and set on fighting just for the experience of it.

She would have told him how insane his plan was, but her name was called again and she had to go.

She won both bouts in the second round, picturing the arms in her head—*ungh-thwap!*—and Noah was as elated with her successes as she was.

"You're a *killer*," he exclaimed, hugging and kissing her after the round. "I wish your dad was here. And Eric. They'd be so proud. You should have let them come, Mich. Oh!" He palmed his forehead. "I should be videotaping this."

His happiness tickled her soul unlike anything she'd known before.

"I haven't won it yet," she reminded him, despite the fact that she was one of the final ten contestants in the women's division. "And the rest of these ladies are pros."

"So what? Your chances are as good as theirs. And just look how far you've made it. That alone is something to be proud of. I'm—"

He stopped short when he was bumped from behind, turning his head to glare over his shoulder. His expression changed to something totally menacing as he moved slightly to reveal the people behind him.

"Well, well, well," he said, smiling tightly at Lola and Jake Carlson. "Look who's here. Come to see what you lost last week?"

Jake, sneaky and underhanded and not easily offended, simply ignored him. Lola, on the other hand, told him exactly and very colorfully what he could do with himself.

"We came because we haven't missed a regional in five years. And we walked all the way back here to wish Mich good luck."

"Right," he said, and then he laughed.

"Lola," Mich said quickly, "I'm glad you came over. Thank you. It means a lot to me."

"No hard feelings, then?" Lola asked.

"No. We've been friends too long for that," she said, leaning forward to give her a small good-sport hug.

"Hey, hey! None of that. Her clothes could be drenched in chloroform."

"Noah . . ."

"You never know, and you can't be too careful," he told her. Turning back to Lola and Jake, he added, "Maybe you two should stand a little more downwind."

He pointed along the rope to where some other female wrestlers were standing. "Or go back where you came from."

"Noah. Now you're being just plain rude."

"Forget it, Mich," Lola said, casting him a dagger-filled glance. "I said what I came over to say. I don't want to stand next to him any longer than I have to anyway."

She turned on her heel and shoved her way back through the crowd. Jake turned to leave, too, but before he did, he muttered, "You're nuts, fella."

"Nuts? Come back here and say that to my face, why don't ya?"

"Noah," she said, grabbing the front of his shirt to get his attention. "You have to stop this."

"Why? I'm just watching out for you. People are capable of all sorts of dirty tricks at times like this."

"Watching out for me?" Good God, what next? "First off, I don't need you to watch out for me. Secondly, Lola wouldn't do anything like that."

"Why? Because she's such a close friend of yours?"

"No," she said honestly. "Because she loves the sport too much."

He supposed he could keep her distracted with an intricate discussion of loving a sport and loving to win, but she started unconsciously bending her arm back and forth, twisting her wrist and flexing her fist.

"Are you all right? How's your arm? Did you hurt it in that last bout? Do you need ice for it?"

"No," she said, glad her own distraction had shifted his attention. "I'm just keeping it warm and loose." She turned a bit to catch the water boy's eye, and he tossed her another bottle of water. "I am sick of all this wait-ing, though."

He could well believe it. With the average tussle taking all of thirty seconds, the standing-around time between matches seemed interminable. But if she was noticing it, he wasn't keeping her busy enough.

"Do you mind?" he asked, his voice full of exaspera-tion as he abruptly turned to a man about his own age that he'd been watching for some time. "Can't you just drink your beer instead of slurping it? The noise you're making is really irritating."

The man looked from Noah to his beer and back again.

"Slurp, slurp, slurp. Where'd you learn to drink like that?"

"You can't possibly hear him drinking over all this noise," Mich said, defending the dazed and confused gentleman. "Even if you could, it's a free country, and he can drink it any way he wants to."

"Oh yeah? You should try standing here, listening to it. It's like a Chinese water torture. Look, pal," he said to the man. "Sorry if I'm being sensitive, but would you mind standing somewhere else?"

Once again the man's gaze passed between Noah and his very silent beer and back before he turned and marched off.

"I don't believe this. Noah, you're out of control."

"I know." He grinned. "Isn't it great?"

"No. It's not. I hate it. And I want it to stop. Now."

"All those years of tolerating bad manners. Suffering through boring conversations. Accepting other people's idiosyncrasies. For the first time in my life I feel completely free."

"You should feel completely ashamed. That poor man . . ."

"That poor man reminds me of me before I met you," he said, watching her beautiful dark eyes go round as saucers. "Meek. Mild. Wussy."

"Mich Albee, representing Albee Trucking Company out of Gypsum, Nevada," they heard the announcer over the loudspeaker. "And Donna James, bodybuilder and personal trainer, Venice Beach, California."

"This conversation isn't over," she told him over her shoulder.

"See it in your head," he called to her back, grinning when she held her thumb in the air.

It was then he saw what he'd been waiting all evening to see. Colossus. Taller than Noah and well over three hundred pounds, he had a beer logo on his shirt stretched bigger than a billboard, long dark hair, narrow eyes . . . he was perfect. Mayhem, pure and clean, bubbled through Noah's veins as he rose on tiptoe to tap the man on the shoulder.

"Excuse me, sir," he said with a big smile. "How would you like to earn a hundred dollars?"

With her win, Mich became one of the five finalists for Southwestern Arm-wrestling Champion.

She and the other onetime loser would match off, and whoever won would go on to wrestle one of the other three—and the winners from those two bouts would vie for the title.

As the contenders became quieter and more intense the crowd went in the opposite direction, growing noiser and noisier.

The building was alive, Mich thought, soaking in the energy. She glanced at Noah, who smiled at her, and she smiled back. She wanted to remember this moment for as long as she lived. Granted, arm wrestling wasn't brain surgery, but at the moment she was one of five who could do something no one else could. On the grand scale of things, it probably didn't matter. But who lived on that grand scale anyway? Ordinary people? John and Jane Doe? The people down the street? No. They lived with smaller, more realistic blueprints of what a good life was, and at the moment Mich's design was pretty close to perfect.

Maybe she should have let Eric and the others come to see what they thought they knew all along, to see her hold her own with the pros, to see her be one of a select few. Someone special.

Her confidence sustained her through the next two bouts, but she could hardly breathe as she took the steps to the stage for the last time to face the Utah state champion, a flight instructor/bodybuilder/mother of two from Provo. Her heart quaked at the woman's stony stare. Her mouth was as dry as a dead man's scalp, and the palms of her hands were numb.

The mother from Provo took hold of the grip, set her elbow, and waited eagerly for Mich to do the same. The woman was too ready, too sure, Mich thought, feeling unready and unsure. She had a spot cleared and dusted on her mantel for the trophy, and Mich didn't.

She took a deep breath, tried to swallow, and stepped up to the table. By rote, she took her stance, grabbed hold of the grip, placed her elbow, and locked grips. In her mind she brought forth the image of the arms, but before she could get a clear picture—*ungh, thwap!*—it was over.

The Utah state champ was now also the new Southwestern Regional Champion, and Mich took second place.

It seemed a little strange to accept congratulations and condolences for the same thing, and to show appreciation for both. Was she supposed to be happy or sad? To be honest, what she felt was . . . nothing. Except perhaps relief that it was over.

Noah, on the other hand, knew what he was feeling. He was still dancing a jig when their gazes met over a small group of people. He held his hands out at his sides and shook his head as if he were awed and speechless.

But of course he wasn't speechless. "You were fantastic. Incredible."

"I lost," she said, walking into his outstretched arms. She felt more than heard the rumble of laughter in his chest.

"You're also impossible," he said, holding her away from him by the shoulders. "Taking second place in your first professional tournament makes you a decided winner, Mich."

She rolled her eyes, gave him a well-maybe shrug and a small smile.

"Come on," he said, stooping to see her face. "Admit it. You're great. Come on."

"Okay," she said, giving in to his enthusiasm.

"No. You have to say it."

She grinned. "I'm great."

"You're terrific."

"I'm terrific."

"We need to celebrate."

"We need to celebrate."

They laughed. He swept her into his arms and kissed her.

"Think this place has champagne?" he asked.

"I'd rather have beer," she said from under his arm as they made their way to the bar.

"Beautiful, smart, an arm-wrestling champion, *and* a cheap date. What more could a man ask for?"

She laughed. "I know what I'd ask for. . . ."

"What?" Her cryptic tone of voice had him craning to see her face; she was smiling when she turned it away. He caught the bartender's attention and ordered two beers, then turned her around to face him. "What?" he asked again, studying her.

She merely stood there, smiling at him, her eyes bright with love and lust, her lips inviting, her head tilted to tease.

With every slow nod of his head his grin grew wider, his eyes wiser. From the beginning of time women had smiled that smile, looked that look to bring men to their knees. He wondered briefly who the idiot was who had labeled them the weaker sex? There was nothing weak or vulnerable about a woman who knew her own heart.

He could count on one hand the times in his life when words had failed him—and this was one of them. There was no smart, pithy remark to razz her with, no sappy, sentimental statement to charm her, no honest terms to describe what he felt. Helpless, he was lost inside her.

He might have stood there the rest of his life, imprinting the image of her at that moment deep in his mind, except that she was suddenly whipped out of view by a pair of long, thick arms.

"Hey!" he shouted as a dark-haired colossus picked her up off the floor and swung her through the air like a paper airplane. "Hey!"

The hulk turned his back on Noah as he hugged Mich like a favorite rag doll. "Congratulations, honey! I had fifty bucks ridin' on you to lose, but that's only 'cuz the other gal was my wife. I was sweatin' the whole time. Ya had me scared, but ya done yourself proud."

"Get your hands off her, you oaf!" Noah said, angrily pulling at the giant's billboard-sized T-shirt. His Hugeness set Mich gently on the floor, then turned his head to peer down at Noah—who threw up his dukes. "Get away from her, or I'll punch your face in."

"Noah, for crying out loud—"

"You may be the ugliest bastard I've ever seen and twice my size, but I don't care. Nobody manhandles my woman."

"Your woman?"

"Well, who does he think he is? Who do you think you are?" he asked the behemoth directly.

Noah imagined the man wasn't much of a fighter. He didn't have to be. All he'd ever have to do is look at someone long enough, and they'd simply disappear—probably in a hurry, most likely leaving a puddle of perspiration behind. But he *was* one hell of an actor. He was looking at Noah as if he were thinking of pinching his head clean off his shoulders.

"I asked you a question, pal. You going to answer me or just stand there looking stupid?"

"Noah. Stop. He was just congratulating me. Having fun."

"Fun?" Noah laughed. "Ha-ha-ha. This is the sort of guy you sit next to when you want to be alone, Mich. Look at him. He's got the personality of the back wall of a racquetball court. Hell, if he fell over and landed on his back, he'd probably break his nose." Then turning back to the oversized man, he added, "Speaking of noses, you wanna lean forward a bit?"

To everyone's surprise the man did lean forward, but not close enough for Noah to take a swing at him. Just close enough to take hold of the front of Noah's shirt and leather vest and lift him straight up off the floor.

From several inches above the mammoth's head, Noah felt a sudden urge to hum a few bars of "On a Clear Day." From that altitude he could see *everthing*. The shock and horror and excitement in the faces of the crowd; Mich, with her hands covering her face; the bartender reaching for the phone and trying to get the bouncer's attention at the same time, and another colossus standing across the room—long dark hair, beer logo on his shirt, a grimace of warning on his face.

Noah looked down slowly. Whoa! Strange how dizzy you could get when all your blood was in your feet, how hard it is to see clearly. Still he saw the ad for

Caterpillar Bulldozers on the front of the man's shirt. Saw that his hair was a bit shorter and lighter than the man he'd given a hundred dollars to. Saw that the anger in the man's face was very, very real. Saw his life flash before his eyes as the man's fist came flying through air at him.

"Oh, Noah," he could hear Mich saying. He couldn't see her, couldn't see anything but the pitch black of night and a few bright stars, fading in and out. "Noah, can you hear me? Say something? Open your eyes, baby. Please. Oh, Noah."

Well . . . it did help to open his eyes a little. He could make out the outline of her crouching form, until she covered his face with something cold and wet, tried to suffocate him with it.

"Lay still, you fool," she said, her voice no longer as concerned as it was angry. "If he didn't break your nose, I will. That was the dumbest thing I've ever seen. You're lucky he didn't kill you."

"Wrong guy," he muttered into the cold compress.

"Well, yeah," she said unsympathetically. "I guess it was the wrong guy."

"What happened?"

"You got your lights punched out. Can you stand up, do you think? I want to get out of here before he changes his mind and comes back."

The thought of that leviathan coming back was enough to get him off the floor, but he needed Mich's strong back to keep him upright. A quick glance around, and he could tell he'd been out long enough to lose most everyone's interest. He stumbled toward the front door in shame.

"That was the dumbest thing I've ever seen," Mich was saying.

"You said that."

"Picking a fight with someone twice your size. Insulting him, not once, but over and over."

"Is my nose bleeding?"

"What if he'd had a weapon? What if he'd wanted to do some *real* damage? Did you even think of that?"

"I think there's blood running down the back of my throat."

"I don't feel sorry for you, you know. You've been asking for that all day," she said. He slipped her a lethal side glance. "You deserved it. I hope this will be the end of this macho nonsense. You're just lucky. . . ."

Noah tried to stand a little straighter as he came up beside the big man who had a hundred extra dollars in his pocket.

"Can I do anything to help?" the man asked, sympathy and regret etched so deeply into his face that Noah wanted to give him another fifty bucks.

"Oh, thanks," Mich said, assuming the man was speaking to her. "But I can handle it. Thanks anyway."

Noah met the man's gentle eyes and shook his head. He tried to smile but found that the left side of his face was numb, so he patted the giant twice on the chest as a gesture of goodwill.

Then, because he couldn't help himself, he burst into laughter. Throwing his head back, his knees buckled, and the big man caught him.

The man she loved was hanging by his armpits in

the hands of a complete stranger, laughing so hard, he couldn't find his own legs. Was he hysterical? Should she slap him? She wanted to slap him, but not necessarily because he was out of his mind. On general principle. Should she be concerned or just stay mad? Let him laugh himself sick? Leave him there in the parking lot laughing like a loon?

She and the stranger exchanged helpless looks and shrugged.

"Just set him down on the curb there. Thanks. He's not normally like this. He's . . . well, I'd tell you what he is, but you'd never believe it. Thanks for helping."

The man said it was no problem, wished them both a good night, and went back inside.

Mich sat down on the curb beside him, crossed her arms over her chest, and said nothing until he was quiet enough to hear her.

"Are you finished?"

"I don't know."

"You better be. I'm so mad I could kill you myself."

"Mad? Why? I was defending you."

"Give me a break. You were looking for a fight, and you got one. And I'm mad because it was not only stupid but you could have gotten hurt."

"I didn't get hurt?" he asked, dabbing at his nose with the wet towel. There didn't seem to be any fresh bleeding, but it still hurt like the devil. "I'll probably look like W. C. Fields the rest of my life, but I'm glad I didn't get hurt."

"It's not even broken, you moron. I wish it had been. Maybe then you'd think twice before you ever pull something like that again. Maybe you'd stop this insane thinking that fighting ever solved anything. If I were that guy, I'd have taught you a *real* lesson. *I'd* have broken your nose for sure. I'd have—"

It might have been the agonizing pain in his nose, or it might have been the toll taken by the last week of putting up with her tricks and taunts, or it might simply have been the right moment to tell her he was completely nuts about her.

"Oh, shut up," he said, angrier than he'd ever known himself to be. "This is all your fault, not mine."

"My fault?"

"Yes. You're the one who said that fighting gets you what you want, that it made you feel great, that *some things* were worth fighting for, that if I wanted you, I'd have to fight for you. Well, honey, I want you. I fought for you. Now look at me."

"I was drunk. I told you to forget all that. I changed my mind."

"Well, I couldn't. And you can't just say something like that and then change your mind. You wanted me to fight for you, and I did. And all I get is more grief." He frowned as something new occurred to him. "You know, come to think of it, *you're* the only one who's ever wanted to fight with me. You're the only one who makes me mad enough to fight. The only one who has something I want. The only person worth fighting with . . ."

He went silent, the challenge clear in his expression.

"You *are* crazy. I'm not going to fight with you."

"Oh yes, you are. Stand up," he said, staggering a bit as he got to his own feet. "You're the only one I really have a beef with, the only one I have to prove anything to. Get up. We're going to settle this, one way or another, once and for all. One-on-one. You and me. Get up."

"No. This is insane. And if you lay one hand on me . . ."

He cursed. "I'm not going to hit you. We'll settle it your way. I'm gonna arm-wrestle you."

"Arm-wrestle me?"

"Yeah. Don't you think I know how? Don't you think you could beat me too? I'm not that much bigger than you, and you're a pro now. You can take me easy. Come on, Mighty Mouth. Get up off your butt and put your arm where your mouth is."

It was true, they were within twenty pounds of each other, and he wasn't experienced. He'd be easier to pull than any one of her brothers.

"All right," she said, getting to her feet at her own speed. "This is as stupid as you are, but if it'll make you happy, name your stakes."

"My stakes?"

She gave him a dry look. "What you want, on the off chance that you win."

"Oh," he said, nodding, thinking hard. He was only going to get one shot at this, and he was going to make it count. "Okay. If I win you have to believe everything I tell you and do whatever I say for the rest of your life."

"What? No way."

"Then just believe everything I tell you."

"No. You're already a known liar. And it can only be one thing. One pull, one thing."

"Okay. But one anything, right?"

Her hesitation was brief. "Yeah. One anything."

"No matter what it is?"

"No matter what it is."

"So if I wrote just one thing down on a piece of paper, and I won, you'd do it, right? Whatever it said."

If he was trying to anger her again with all this hair-splitting, he was succeeding.

"Didn't I say anything, no matter what?"

"I'm just checking." He started rolling his shoulder muscles and flexing his arm. "We need paper."

"Oh! For—" She stopped herself. "We can just say what we want."

That hadn't been Noah's experience with her to date.

"No. It'll be more exciting if we write it down and keep it secret. More at stake. More to win."

Like trust.

She rolled her eyes and marched back into the bar, returning seconds later with a pen and two Eddy's napkins.

"This is ridiculous," she said, pen poised. "Everything is always so complicated with you. It can't be a simple arm pull, it has"—he was already finished with his secret bet, slapping it down on the hood of the car next to them—". . . it has to have secret bets and super-deluxe rules."

"Yeah, yeah. Hurry up. My nose hurts," he said, testing the bridge of it for swelling.

Mich eyed his napkin, wondering what it was he could be so quick to ask of her. What he wanted from her so badly that he'd thought it out ahead of time.

Actually, her request was just as easy for her to decide upon. Four simple words—no, the last two were a compound word. She hooked them together.

"Okay," she said, trying to sound confident and careless. She folded her napkin and slapped it down on the hood of the car atop his. "Enough rigmarole. Put up or shut up."

He gave her a narrow-eyed grimace of disdain, bent at the waist, and set his elbow on the hood of the car.

"I'm here waitin' for ya, fancy-pants. Let me know when you're done runnin' your mouth."

She simpered for him, leaned against the car, and gave him her arm. They stared each other in the eye, the neon lights from the bar reflecting their resolve and determination. This was an arm wrestle to the death, neither of them willing to give an inch—both intent on collecting their prize.

Glaring with clenched teeth, they locked grips.

"On three?" he asked, and she shrugged her consent.

"One."

"Two."

"Three."

Biceps bulged. Faces contorted with exertion. Stances were quickly adjusted. She grunted. He groaned. The teepeed arms wavered minutely, vibrated with the tension, but didn't really lean in one direction or the other. He grunted. She groaned. Knuckles turned white. Fingers squirmed for a dominant position. The arms shook, pointing skyward.

Thirty seconds slipped into forty-five. Ninety seconds became two whole minutes. Muscles twitched with fatigue. Stances were readjusted, facial expressions renewed. He grumbled. She griped. The clasp teetered an inch to the right, then an inch to the left; another inch to the left, then an inch to the right.

Three minutes and the arms began to tingle. Muscles jumped spasmodically.

"This is stupid," she said between her teeth.

"Give up?"

"No. Never."

"You look tired," he suggested.

"You look like hell. Your nose is bleeding again."

He frowned and would have reached up to check but didn't dare let himself be distracted. "Nice try, but I'll bleed to death before I let you win this."

"I can wait," she said.

"Ha! That's sweet. If you were bleeding, I'd offer a draw."

She lifted a single brow as if to say, "Well that's you, not me." Then she said, "I thought you wanted this settled. Once and for all."

"I do. I'd just rather not bleed out before I can collect."

She snorted—as if he'd be collecting anything anyway.

"Listen. I'm prepared to stand here till dawn if I have to," he said.

"Then why don't you give up now and save us both some time?"

"Very funny. But I can tell your arm's hurting. I can see it in your eyes."

"So? Yours is too. It has to be." She grunted to restore some of her stamina.

"It is. But I was thinking of going to a hospital to

get my nose checked anyway. If I break anything, I'll have it all taken care of at once."

She couldn't stare at him any longer, she just couldn't. She leaned her head against the rock-hard arms and sighed. Glancing over at the two napkins, she said, "You know, we could end this and both of us get what we want."

"How?"

"We could . . . read the stakes. Agree to whatever they say. Call it even." She raised her head to look at him.

"At the same time? Read them together? Agree together? Let go at the same time?"

"Yeah. Sound fair to you?"

His eyes narrowed and his lips twitched as he thought about it. "Yeah. That sounds fair."

Slowly and silently they each reached with their free hand to take one of the napkins. They looked at each other one more time before opening them and focusing on the notes. They frowned at the same time, and their gazes met in confusion.

"I got mine," he said, turning it so she could read.

"Me too," she said, turning hers to him.

The light in their eyes shone through with comprehension. Mich started to giggle, and Noah's laughter echoed across the tips of the San Francisco peaks.

Still locked palm to palm, they pressed their aching arms between them as they came together in the embrace they'd fought so hard for. Their lips met in a kiss that was both a beginning and an end, the first of many kisses, with the passion of a last kiss.

They didn't see the shooting star that crossed the

sky above them. They didn't hear the lark singing lulla-
bies to her babies, high in the eaves of Eddy's. They
didn't feel the gentle breeze that pulled at single strands
of their hair and tugged at the corners of the napkins on
the hood of the car.

The napkins on which they'd written the same three
simple words—*love me forever*.

Cool air brushed across the overwarm flesh of her
back and abdomen when he pulled her shirttail from the
waistband of her jeans. His hands were hot and eager.

"Noah," she said, when the shirt rose higher and
higher. She peeled her lips away from his and pushed
feebly against his chest. "We can't. Not here."

He kissed her again, paid her no heed. She kissed
him back.

Gasping and laughing, she pulled away again. She'd
be lucky if they made it to the truck for a little privacy.

"There's a nice big bed back at the motel," she said,
enticing him. "Two in fact. Let's wait till we get back to
the motel."

"Huh-ha," he mumbled with his lips on her neck. In
a calculated motion, his hands slid up her back, leaving
gooseflesh in their wake. He snapped the hook on her
bra.

"Noah," she said, breathing the word out on a sigh
of weakness when his hands closed over her breast to
gently knead and excite. "Noah, wait."

"Mmm," he said between nibbles at her neck. "I've
waited too long already. I want you. I fought for you.
You're mine now."

"Yes, I am. Now and forever," she said. "Let's go
back to the motel and I'll show you."

"Show me now."

He bent his head as he pushed her shirt higher over her breasts, to get to them with his mouth. She grabbed the shirt and pulled it down as close to her knees as she could.

"Nope," she said, grinning, scooting back toward the truck, dragging him with her, an ardent prisoner.

She bumped into a parked car, and he took the opportunity to kiss her, long and deep. The fog in her head cleared a bit when she felt the button give way on her jeans and his shaky hands fumbling with the zipper. A quick glance about and she spotted the truck within dashing distance.

"Noah. Noah, your hat. You left your hat inside," she said, using the urgency churning wildly inside her to get his attention. The ruse worked, and when he looked up in confusion—his hands going automatically to where his hat should have been—she grabbed the front of her pants and ran.

"You don't play fair," he called, following her.

"Of course, I do. An Albee is nothing if not—"

"Yeah, yeah. . . . fair," he said, catching her as she reached for the door handle on the truck. "And what will you be when you become a Tessler?"

She looped her arms around his neck and pecked at his lips.

"Then I'll be your wife and *everything* will be fair."

He laughed, and while holding her close, he swatted her backside. "Two can play that game, you know."

"Ha! Mr. Law-abiding-citizen-foreign-diplomat-perfectly proper-hyperhonest-straight-as-an-arrow-permanent-crease-in-his-khaki-pants-peacemaking"—his hands fell from her hips and went akimbo to his, waiting for her to finish—"people-loving-neat-freak-computer-literate-supersexy-sweet-as-can-be Tessler? I don't think so," she said, opening the truck door and climbing in before he could grasp the last two names.

"Come here and say that, honey," he said, following her into the cab of the truck in a predatory fashion. She began to giggle with nerves. She wiggled across the seat until she was wedged between the steering wheel, the seat, and the door. Flushed, anxious, and eager, she held her breath as she watched him stalk her. "Talk big now, why don't ya? Huh? Just remember, you're not dealing with a sane man anymore. I wear jeans and boots and get beat up in bars now."

"Oh. Right. I forgot," she said, splaying her hands across his chest, pretending to keep him at bay.

"Need a reminder?"

"Well . . . maybe just a little refresher course," she murmured, even as his mouth covered hers.

She grappled with the steering wheel to embrace him. He had one knee on the seat and the other teetering painfully on the handle of a cooler on the floor. He rammed his fingers against the armrest trying to hold her. She bonked her head on the door in an attempt to sink lower on the seat.

After several minutes of leg flailing and elbow bumping, their passions steaming, bodies aching with need, Noah swore colorfully and they started to laugh.

"How do people do this?" Mich wondered.

"Beats me, but we definitely need a bed. Move over, I'll drive."

He redefined the term *bat out of hell* in the few short

blocks back to the motel. The light at the corner had just turned red, and cars blocked the entrance to the parking lot. Without stopping, and barely slowing down, he jumped the curb and the grassy parking strip, halting on a dime in their usual parking space.

"Ha! I'm outta control." He chortled happily, scrambling out of the truck. She laughed, feeling a little out of control herself, and pulled on the door handle. "No, no. Wait there. Don't get out yet," he said, rounding the front of the truck.

He came to the door and opened it wide, extending a hand to her. She turned on the seat thinking he was going to help her out in a grand gentlemanly fashion. But when he put his hands about her waist and she leaned forward to get down, he hoisted her up and slung her over his shoulder as if she were a sack of potatoes.

"I've always wanted to do this," he shouted over her laughing protests. "I thought about using a club and dragging you in by your hair, but then I'd have to wait for you to come to before I could ravish you. I love this new me."

"Yes, yes, but I love the old you," she said as they passed through the door.

"You do?" He stopped outside the door to her room and smiled. "So you like the creases in my pants?"

"Yes. I do."

"And I don't have to fight anymore?"

"No. No more."

"And it's okay that I come from a privileged back-ground?"

"Sure."

"So I'm not a spoiled rich kid."

"Absolutely not."

"And you like my new brown hat."

Silence.

His grin broadened as he let her slide slowly down his body to the floor in front of him. Her deep brown eyes were happy and bright when she looked up into his. His chest ached as he recognized the rest of his life through the windows to her soul.

He lowered his mouth to hers and kissed her until the building swayed around them.

"I love everything about you," he said, his lips brushing against hers. "But most of all, I love that you love me."

"I do," she whispered, deepening the kiss as she reached into the back pocket of her jeans for the room key. "I do love you."

No ordinary key, she thought, holding it up for him to see. This key unlocked the door to her every wish, her smallest dreams, her silliest feminine fantasies. This key opened the way to her future.

THE EDITORS'
CORNER

Ladies, step back! This July, LOVESWEPT is hotter than ever, with a month full of beguiling heroes and steamy romance. We managed to capture four Rebels with a Cause for your reading pleasure. There's Jack, a rough-and-tough detective with a glint in his eye; Luke, an architect who has to prove his innocence to win the heart of his woman; Clint, an FBI renegade with a score to settle; and Mitch, an ex–Navy Seal who's determined to earn back the life he left behind.

Beautiful Alex Sheridan and sexy Luke Morgan pack a lifetime of passion into **JUST ONE NIGHT,** LOVESWEPT #898, Eve Gaddy's sexy tale of two strangers who are trying to forget the past. As an officer on the Dallas bomb squad, Alex is called in to investigate the bombing of a construction site. All leads point to Luke, the architect on the project: he's a trained explosives expert; a large amount of money mysteriously shows up in his account; *and* he's the son of a convicted terrorist. As the hunt for the bomber continues, Alex and Luke are in too deep to keep their relationship on a professional basis. Alex had feared she'd never be able to trust herself again, but will Luke convince her that her instincts about him are right? Eve Gaddy pulls at the heartstrings in this moving story of a man who's backed against a wall and the woman who's willing to risk everything to save him.

In **A SCENT OF EDEN**, LOVESWEPT #899, Cynthia Powell demonstrates the delicious power of unlikely attractions. When Eden Wellbourne's fiancé goes missing, it's up to her to find the culprit. To that end, she hires Jack Rafferty, a man who is reputed to have an unmatched expertise in locating missing persons, a man who is clearly living on the edge. Meanwhile, Jack is having the second-worst day of his life, and he's definitely not in the mood to deal with the uptown girl standing on his doorstep. With his cash flow at an all-time low, however, he reluctantly decides to take on her case. Both are confused at the physical pull they feel toward each other, but neither wants to act on it first. When a break-in convinces Eden her own life is in danger, she turns to Jack for more than just his people-finding talents. Everything comes up roses when Cynthia Powell crosses a down-on-his-luck tough guy with a perfume princess.

Next, Jill Shalvis offers **LOVER COME BACK**, LOVESWEPT #900. As the editor of the *Heather Bay Daily News*, Justine Miller makes it her business to know what's happening in her town. But nothing could have prepared her for the shock of seeing her long-lost husband again. Not to mention the fact that he's the proud new owner of her newspaper. Two years earlier, Justine had anxiously waited for her new husband to return to their honeymoon suite. Only, Mitch Conner had disappeared, leaving Justine to deal with the embarrassment and pain. Mitch had had no choice but to leave her, but now he's back and more than eager to reclaim the love of his life. Justine refuses to believe his cockamamy story of corruption and witness protection programs. She has had her taste of marriage and love, and she's through with it. Mitch faces the toughest assignment of his life—proving to her that he'll never leave her. Jill Shalvis delivers a story of true love that can stand the test of time.

Finally, Karen Leabo brings us **THE DEVIL AND THE DEEP BLUE SEA,** LOVESWEPT #901. FBI agent Clint Nichols has a plan. Not a well-thought-out plan, but a plan nonetheless. He's going to kidnap a sister to exchange for an ex-wife. But the minute he boards the *Fortune's Smile*, Clint knows this mission will be a bust. His pretty quarry, Marissa Gabriole, pulls a gun on him and his getaway boat sinks. He's also hampered by a hurricane on the way and an accomplice who's a moron. Marissa soon grows tired of being on the run and chooses to team up with her kidnapper to flush out a mob boss. Clint isn't sure whether he can trust Marissa, but he knows it's the only way to wrap up an extensive undercover operation. Besides, what more does he have to lose? His life, for one thing. His heart, for another. Karen Leabo expertly blurs the line between what's right and what's love in this fast-paced, seaworthy caper.

Happy reading!

Susann Brailey

Joy Abella

Susann Brailey

Joy Abella

Senior Editor

Administrative Editor